# HUNTING THE LIONS

**R.M. BALLANTYNE**

*Frontispiece by John Betancourt. Based on a painting.*

# HUNTING THE LIONS

## R.M. Ballantyne

**WILDSIDE PRESS**

# HUNTING THE LIONS

# INTRODUCTION

Robert Michael Ballantyne (1825–1894) was a Scottish author who published more than 100 books. He was also an accomplished artist and exhibited some of his water-colours at the Royal Scottish Academy.

Ballantyne was born in Edinburgh, the ninth of ten children (and the youngest son), to Alexander and Anne Ballantyne. His father was a newspaper editor and printer in the family firm of "Ballantyne & Co" based at Paul's Works on the Canongate. His uncle, James Ballantyne, was the printer for Scottish author Sir Walter Scott. A banking crisis in 1825 resulted in the collapse of the Ballantyne printing business the following year with debts of £130,000,which led to a decline in the family's fortunes.

Robert Ballantyne went to Canada at the age of 16 and spent five years working for the Hudson's Bay Company. He traded with the local Native Americans for furs, which required him to travel by canoe and sleigh to the areas occupied by the modern-day provinces of Manitoba, Ontario, and Quebec—experiences that formed the basis of his novel *Snowflakes and Sunbeams* (1856). His longing for family and home during that period impressed him to start writing letters to his mother. Ballantyne recalled in his autobiographical *Personal Reminiscences in Book Making* (1893) that "To this long-letter writing I attribute whatever small amount of facility in composition I may have acquired."

In 1847 Ballantyne returned to Scotland to discover that his father had died. He published his first book the following year, *Hudson's Bay: or, Life in the Wilds of North America*, and for some time was employed by the publishers Messrs Constable. In 1856 he gave up business to focus on his literary career and began the series of adventure stories for the young with which his name is popularly associated.

*The Young Fur-Traders* (1856), *The Coral Island* (1857), *The World of Ice* (1859), *Ungava: a Tale of Eskimo Land* (1857), *The Dog*

*Crusoe* (1860), *The Lighthouse* (1865), *Fighting the Whales* (1866), *Deep Down* (1868), *The Pirate City* (1874), *Erling the Bold* (1869), *The Settler and the Savage* (1877), and more than 100 other books followed in regular succession, his rule being to write as far as possible from personal knowledge of the scenes he described. *The Gorilla Hunters: A tale of the wilds of Africa* (1861) shares three characters with The Coral Island: Jack Martin, Ralph Rover and Peterkin Gay. Here Ballantyne relied factually on Paul du Chaillu's Exploration in Equatorial Guinea, which had appeared early in the same year.

*The Coral Island* remains the most popular of the Ballantyne novels still read and remembered today, but because of a mistake he made in that book—he gave an incorrect thickness of coconut shells—he prioritized research on his subjects for later books. For instance, he spent time living with the lighthouse keepers at the Bell Rock before writing *The Lighthouse*, and he spent time with the tin miners of Cornwall while researching *Deep Down*.

In 1866 he married Jane Grant, with whom he had three sons and three daughters. He spent his later years in Harrow, London, before moving to Italy for the sake of his health, possibly suffering from undiagnosed Ménière's disease. He died in Rome in 1894 and was buried in the Protestant Cemetery there.

One of the young men influenced by Ballantyne's novels was Robert Louis Stevenson (1850–94). Stevenson was so impressed with the story of *The Coral Island* (1857) that he based portions of his most famous book, *Treasure Island* (1881), on themes found in Ballantyne's classic novel.

—Karl Wurf
Rockville, Maryland

# CHAPTER I.

### Begins to Unfold the Tale of the Lions by Describing the Lion of the Tale.

We trust, good reader, that it will not cause you a feeling of disappointment to be told that the name of our hero is Brown — Tom Brown. It is important at the beginning of any matter that those concerned should clearly understand their position, therefore we have thought fit, even at the risk of throwing a wet blanket over you, to commence this tale on one of the most romantic of subjects by stating — and now repeating that our hero was a member of the large and (supposed to be) unromantic family of "the Browns."

A word in passing about the romance of the family. Just because the Brown family is large, it has some to be deemed unromantic. Every one knows that two of the six green-grocers in the next street are Browns. The fat sedate butcher round the corner is David Brown, and the milkman is James Brown. The latter is a square-faced practical man, who is looked up to as a species of oracle by all his friends. Half a dozen drapers within a mile of you are named Brown, and all of them are shrewd men of business, who have feathered their nests well, and stick to business like burrs. You will certainly find that several of the hardest-working clergymen, and one or more of the city missionaries, are named Brown; and as to Doctor Browns, there is no end of them! But why go further? The fact is patent to every unprejudiced person.

Now, instead of admitting that the commonness of the name of Brown proves its owners to be unromantic, we hold that this is a distinct evidence of the deep-seated romance of the family. In the first place, it is probable that their multitudinosity is the result of romance, which, as every one knows, has a tendency to cause men and women to fall in love, and marry early in life. Brown is almost always a good husband and a kind father. Indeed he is a good, steady-going man in all the relations of life, and his name, in our mind at least, is generally associated with troops of happy children who call him "daddy," and regard him in the light of an elephantine playmate. And they do so with good reason, for Brown is manly and thorough-going in whatever he undertakes, whether it be the transaction of business or romping with his children.

But, besides this, the multitudinosity of the Browns cuts in two directions. If there are so many of them green-grocers, butchers, and milkmen — who without sufficient reason are thought to be unromantic — it will be found that they are equally numerous in other walks of life; and wherever they walk they do so coolly, deliberately, good-humouredly, and very practically. Look at the learned professions, for instance. What a host of Browns are there. The engineers and contractors too, how they swarm in their lists. If you want to erect a suspension bridge over the British Channel, the only man who is likely to undertake the job for you is Adam Brown, C.E., and Abel Brown will gladly provide the materials. As to the army, here their name is legion; they compose an army of themselves; and they are all enthusiasts — but quiet, steady-going, not noisy or boastful enthusiasts. In fact, the romance of Brown consists very much in his willingness to fling himself, heart and soul, into whatever his hand finds to do. The man who led the storming party, and achieved immortal glory by getting himself riddled to death with bullets, was Lieutenant Brown — better known as Ned Brown by his brother officers, who could not mention his name without choking for weeks after his sad but so-called "glorious" fall. The other man who accomplished the darling wish of his heart — to win the Victoria Cross — by attaching a bag of gunpowder to the gate of the fortress and blowing it and himself to atoms to small that no shred of him big enough to hang the Victoria Cross upon was ever found, was Corporal Brown, and there was scarcely a dry eye in the regiment when he went down.

Go abroad among the barbarians of the earth, to China, for instance, and ask who is yonder thick-set, broad-chested man, with the hearty expression of face, and the splendid eastern uniform, and you will be told that he is Too Foo, the commander-in-chief of the Imperial forces in that department. If, still indulging curiosity, you go and introduce yourself to him, he will shake you heartily by the hand, and, in good English, tell you that his name is Walter Brown, and that he will be charmed to show you something of Oriental life if you will do him the favour to take a slice of puppy dog in his pagoda after the review! If there is a chief of a hill tribe in Hindustan in want of a prime minister who will be able to carry him through a serious crisis, there is a Brown at hand, who speaks not only his own language, but all the dialects and languages of Hindustan, who is quite ready to assume office. It is the same at the diggings, whether of Australia, California, or Oregon; and we are persuaded that the man whose habitation is nearest to the pole at this moment, whether north or south, is a Brown, if he be not a Jones, Robinson, or Smith!

Need more be said to prove that this great branch of the human family is truly associated with all that is wild, grand, and romantic? We think not; and we hope that the reader is now somewhat reconciled to the fact — which cannot be altered, and which we would not alter if we could — that our hero's name is

Tom Brown.

Tom was the son of a settler at the Cape of Good Hope, who, after leading the somewhat rough life of a trader into the interior of Africa, made a fortune, and retired to a suburban villa in Cape Town, there to enjoy the same with his wife and family. Having been born in Cape Town, our hero soon displayed a disposition to extend his researches into the unknown geography of his native land, and on several occasions lost himself in the bush. Thereafter he ran away from school twice, having been seized with a romantic and irresistible desire to see and shoot a lion! In order to cure his son of this propensity, Mr. Brown sent him to England, where he was put to school, became a good scholar, and a proficient in all games and athletic exercises. After that he went to college, intending, thereafter, to return to the Cape, join his father, and go on a trading expedition into the interior, in order that he might learn the business, and carry it on for himself.

Tom Brown's mother and sisters — there were six of the latter — were charming ladies. Everybody said what pleasant people the Browns were — that there was no nonsense about them, and that they were so practical, yet so lively and full of spirit. Mrs. Brown, moreover, actually held the belief that people had souls as well as bodies, which required feeding in order to prevent starvation, and ensure healthy growth! On the strength of this belief she fed her children out of that old-fashioned, yet ever new, volume, the Bible, and the consequence was, that the Miss Browns were among the most useful members of the church to which they belonged, a great assistance to the clergymen and missionaries who waited those regions, and a blessing to the poor of the community. But we must dismiss the family without further remark, for our story has little or nothing to do with any member of it except Tom himself.

When he went to school in England, Tom carried his love

for the lion along with him. The mere word had a charm for him which he could not account for. In childhood he had dreamed of lion-hunting; in riper years he played at games of his own invention which had for their chief point the slaying or capturing of lions. Zoological gardens and "wild beast shows" had for him attractions which were quite irresistible. As he advanced in years, Richard of the Lion-heart became his chief historical hero; Androcles and the lion stirred up all the enthusiasm of his nature. Indeed it might have been said that the lion-rampant was stamped indelibly on his heart, while the British lion became to him the most attractive myth on record.

When he went to college and studied medicine, his imagination was sobered down a little; but when he had passed his examinations and was capped, and was styled Dr. Brown by his friends, and began to make preparations for going back to the Cape, all his former enthusiasm about lions returned with tenfold violence.

Tom's father intended that he should study medicine, not with a view to practising it professionally, but because he held it to be very desirable that every one travelling in the unhealthy regions of South Africa should possess as much knowledge of medicine as possible.

One morning young Dr. Brown received a letter from his father which ran as follows: —

"*My dear Tom*, —
        "A capital opportunity of letting you see a little of the country in which I hope you will ultimately make your fortune has turned up just now. Two officers of the Cape Rifles have made up their minds to go on a hunting excursion into the interior with a trader named Hicks, and want a third man to join them. I knew you would like to go on such an expedition, remembering your leaning in that direction in days of old, so I

have pledged you to them. As they start three months hence, the sooner you come out the better. I enclose a letter of credit to enable you to fit out and start at once. Your mother and sisters are all well, and send love.

"— *Your affectionate father, J.B.*"

Tom Brown uttered a wild cheer of delight on reading this brief and business-like epistle, and his curious landlady immediately answered to the shout by entering and wishing to know "if he had called and if he wanted hanythink?"

"No, Mrs. Pry, I did not call; but I ventured to express my feelings in regard to a piece of good news which I have just received."

"La, sir!"

"Yes, Mrs. Pry, I'm going off immediately to South Africa to hunt lions."

"You *don't* mean it, sir!"

"Indeed I do, Mrs. Pry; so pray let me have breakfast without delay, and make up my bill to the end of the week; I shall leave you then. Sorry to part, Mrs. Pry. I have been very comfortable with you."

"I 'ope so, sir."

"Yes, very comfortable; and you may be assured that I shall recommend your lodgings highly wherever I go — not that there is much chance of my recommendation doing you any good, for out in the African bush I sha'n't see many men who want furnished lodgings in London, and wild beasts are not likely to make inquiries, being already well provided in that way at home. By the way, when you make up your bill, don't forget to charge me with the tumbler I smashed yesterday in making chemical experiments, and the tea-pot cracked in the same good cause. Accidents will happen, you know, Mrs. Pry, and bachelors are bound to pay for 'em."

"Certainly, sir; and please, sir, what am I to do with the cup-board full of skulls and 'uman bones downstairs?"

"Anything you choose, Mrs. Pry," said Tom, laughing; "I shall trouble my head no more with such things, so you may sell them if you please, or send them as a valuable gift to the British Museum, only don't bother me about them; and do take yourself off like a good soul, for I must reply to my father's letter immediately."

Mrs. Pry retired, and Tom Brown sat down to write a letter to "J.B." in which he briefly thanked him for the letter of credit, and assured him that one of the dearest wishes of his heart was about to be realised, for that still — not less but rather more than when he was a runaway boy — his soul was set upon hunting the lions.

# CHAPTER III.

### In which Great Deeds are Done, and Tom Brown has a Narrow Escape.

But Tom was wrong. Either the report had been false, or the lions had a special intimation that certain destruction approached them; for our hunters waited two nights at the native kraal without seeing one, although the black king thereof stoutly affirmed that they had attacked the cattle enclosures nearly every night for a week past, and committed great havoc.

One piece of good fortune, however, attended them, which was that they unexpectedly met with the large party which the major had expressed his wish to join. It consisted of about thirty men, four of whom were sportsmen, and the rest natives, with about twenty women and children, twelve horses, seventy oxen, five wagons, and a few dogs; all under the leadership of a trader named Hardy.

Numerous though the oxen were, there were not too many of them, as the reader may easily believe when we tell him that the wagons were very large, clumsy, and heavily laden, — one of them, besides other things, carrying a small boat — and that it occasionally required the powers of twenty oxen to drag one wagon up some of the bad hills they encountered on the journey to the Zulu country.

The four sportsmen, who were named respectively Pearson, Ogilvie, Anson, and Brand, were overjoyed at the addition to the party of Tom Brown and his companions, the more so that Tom was a doctor, for the constitutions of two of them, Ogilvie and Anson, had proved to be scarcely capable of withstanding the evil effects of the climate. Tom prescribed for them so successfully that they soon regained their strength; a result which he believed, however, was fully as much due to the cheering effects of the addition to their social circle as to medicine.

Having rested at the kraal a few days, partly to recruit the travellers, and partly to give the lions an opportunity of returning and being shot, the whole band set forth on their journey to the Umveloose river, having previously rendered the king of the kraal and his subjects happy by a liberal present of beads, brass wire, blue calico, and blankets.

At the kraal they had procured a large quantity of provisions for the journey — amobella meal for porridge, mealies, rice, beans, potatoes, and water-melons; and, while there, they had enjoyed the luxury of as much milk as they could drink; so that all the party were in pretty good condition and excellent spirits when they left. But this did not last very long, for the weather suddenly changed, and rain fell in immense quantities. The long rank grass of those regions became so saturated that it was impossible to keep one's-self dry; and, to add to their discomforts, mosquitoes increased in numbers to such an extent that some of the European travellers could scarcely obtain a wink of sleep.

"Oh dear!" groaned poor Wilkins, one night as he lay between the major and Tom Brown on the wet grass under the shelter of a bullock-wagon covered with a wet blanket; "how I wish that the first mosquito had never been born!"

"If the world could get on without rain," growled the major, "my felicity would be complete. There is a particular stream which courses down the underside of the right shaft of the wagon, and meets with some obstruction just at the point which causes it to pour continuously down my neck. I've shifted my position twice, but it appears to follow me, and I have had sensations for the last quarter of an hour which induce me to believe that a rivulet is bridged by the small of my back. Ha! have you killed him this time?"

The latter remark was addressed to Tom Brown, who had for some time past been vigorously engaged slapping his own face in the vain hope of slaying his tormentors — vain, not only because they were too quick to be caught in that way, but also, because, if slain by hundreds at every blow, there would still have remained thousands more to come on!

"No," replied Tom, with a touch of bitterness in his tone; "he's not dead yet."

"He?" exclaimed Wilkins; "do you mean to say that you are troubled by only *one* of the vile creatures?"

"Oh no!" said Tom; "there are millions of 'em humming viciously round my head at this moment, but one of them is so big and assiduous that I have come to recognise his voice — there! d'you hear it?"

"Hear it!" cried Wilkins; "how can you expect me to hear one of yours when I am engaged with a host of my own? Ah! but I hear *that*," he added, laughing, as another tremendous crack resounded from Tom Brown's cheek; "what a tough skin you must have, to be sure, to stand such treatment?"

"I am lost in admiration of the amiableness of your temper, Tom," remarked the major. "If I were to get such a slap in the face as that, even from myself, I could not help flying in a passion. Hope the enemy is defeated at last?"

"I — I—think so," said Tom, in that meditative tone which assures the listener that the speaker is intensely on the *qui vive*; "yes, I believe I *have* — eh—no — there he — oh!"

Another pistol-shot slap concluded the sentence, and poor Tom's companions in sorrow burst into a fit of laughter.

"Let 'im bite, sir," growled the deep bass voice of Hardy, who lay under a neighbouring wagon; "when he's got his beak well shoved into you, and begins to suck, he can't get away so quick, 'cause of havin' to pull it out again! hit out hard and quick then, an' you're sure of him. But the best way's to let 'em bite, an' go to sleep."

"Good advice; I'll try to take it," said Tom, turning round with a sigh, and burying his face in the blanket. His companions followed his example, and in spite of rain and mosquitoes were soon fast asleep.

This wet weather had a very depressing effect on their spirits, and made the region so unhealthy that it began ere long to tell on the weaker members of the sporting party; as for the natives, they, being inured to it, were proof against everything. Being all but naked, they did not suffer from wet garments; and as they smeared their bodies over with grease, the rain ran off them as it does off the ducks. However, it did not last long at that time. In a few days the sky cleared, and the spirits of the party revived with their health.

The amount of animal life seen on the journey was amazing. All travellers in Africa have borne testimony to the fact that it teems with animals. The descriptions which, not many years ago, were deemed fabulous, have been repeated to us as sober truth by men of unquestionable veracity. Indeed, no description, however vivid, can convey to those whose personal experience has been limited to the fields of Britain an adequate conception of the teeming millions of living creatures, great and small, four-footed and winged, which swarm in the dense forests and mighty plains of the African wilderness.

Of course the hunters of the party were constantly on the alert, and great was the slaughter done; but great also was the capacity of the natives for devouring animal food, so that very little of the sport could be looked upon in the light of life taken in vain.

Huge and curious, as well as beautiful, were the creatures "bagged."

On one occasion Tom Brown went out with the rest of the party on horseback after some elephants, the tracks of which had been seen the day before. In the course of the day Tom was separated from his companions, but being of an easy-going disposition, and having been born with a thorough belief in the impossibility of anything very serious happening to him, he was not much alarmed, and continued to follow what he thought were the tracks of elephants, expecting every moment to fall in with, or hear shots from his friends.

During the journey Tom had seen the major, who was an old sportsman, kill several elephants, so that he conceived himself to be quite able for that duty if it should devolve upon him. He was walking his horse quietly along a sort of path that skirted a piece of thicket when he heard a tremendous crashing of trees, and looking up saw a troop of fifty or sixty elephants dashing away through a grove of mapani-trees. Tom at once put spurs to his horse, unslung his large-bore double-barrelled gun, and coming close up to a cow-elephant, sent a ball into her behind the shoulder. She did not drop, so he gave her another shot, when she fell heavily to the ground.

At that moment he heard a shot not far off. Immediately afterwards there was a sound of trampling feet which rapidly increased, and in a few moments the whole band of elephants came rushing back towards him, having been turned by the major with a party of natives. Not having completed the loading of his gun, Tom hastily rode behind a dense bush, and concealed himself as well as he could. The herd turned aside just before reaching the bush, and passed him about a hundred yards off with a tremendous rush, their trunks and tails in the air, and the major and Wilkins, with a lot of natives and dogs, in full pursuit. Tom was beginning to regret that he had not fired a long shot at them, when he heard a crash behind him, and looking back saw a monstrous bull-elephant making a terrific charge at him. It was a wounded animal, mad with rage and pain, which had caught sight of him in passing. Almost before he was aware of its approach it went crashing through the thicket trumpeting furiously, and tearing down trees, bushes, and everything before it.

Tom lay forward on the neck of his steed and drove the spurs into him. Away they went like the wind with the elephant close behind. In his anxiety Tom cast his eyes too often behind him. Before he could avoid it he was close on the top of a very steep slope, or stony hill, which went down about fifty yards to the plain below. To rein up was impossible, to go down would have been almost certain death to horse and man. With death before and behind, our hero had no alternative but to swerve, for the trunk of the huge creature was already almost over the haunch of his terrified horse. He did swerve. Pulling the horse on his haunches, and swinging him round at the same moment as if on a pivot, he made a bound to the left. The elephant passed him with a shriek like that of a railway engine, stuck out its feet before it, and went sliding wildly down the slope — as little boys are sometimes wont to do — sending dust, atones, and rubbish in a stupendous cloud before him. At the foot he lost his balance, and the last that Tom saw of him was a flourish of his stumpy tail as he went heels over head to the bottom of the hill. But he could not stop to see more; his horse was away with him, and fled over the plain on the wings of terror for a mile in the opposite direction before he consented to be pulled up.

Tom's companions, meanwhile, had shot two elephants — one a cow, the other a pretty old calf, and on their way back to camp they killed a buffalo. The other hunters had been also successful, so that the camp resounded with noisy demonstrations of joy, and the atmosphere ere long became redolent of the fumes of roasting meat, while the black bodies of the natives absolutely glittered with grease.

On summing up the result of the day's work, it was found that they had bagged six elephants, three elands, two buffaloes, and a variety of smaller game.

"A good bag," observed the major as he sipped his tea; "but I have seen better. However, we must rest content. By the way, Pearson, they tell me you had a narrow escape from a buffalo-bull."

"So I had," replied Pearson, pausing in the midst of a hearty meal that he was making off a baked elephant's foot; "but for Anson there I believe it would have been my last hunt."

"How did he help you?" asked Tom Brown.

"Come, tell them, Anson, you know best," said Pearson; "I am too busy yet to talk."

"Oh, it was simple enough," said Anson with a laugh. "He and I had gone off together after a small herd of buffaloes; Ogilvie and Brand were away following up the spoor of an elephant. We came upon the buffaloes unexpectedly, and at the first shot Pearson dropped one dead — shot through the heart. We were both on foot, having left our horses behind, because the ground was too stony for them. After a hard chase of two hours we came up with the herd. Pearson fired at a young bull and broke its leg, nevertheless it went off briskly on the remaining three, so I fired and shot off its tail. This appeared to tickle his fancy, for he turned at once and charged Pearson, who dropped his gun, sprang into a thorn-tree and clambered out of reach only just in time to escape the brute, which grazed his heel in passing. Poor fellow, he got such a fright —"

"False!" cried Pearson, with his mouth full of meat.

" — that he fell off the tree," continued Anson, "and the bull turned to charge again, so, out of pity for my friend, I stopped him with a bullet in the chest."

"It was well done, Anson, I'm your debtor for life," said Pearson, holding out his plate; "just give me a little more of that splendid foot and you'll increase the debt immeasurably; you see the adventure has not taken away my appetite."

As he said this a savage growl was heard close to the wagon beside which they were seated. It was followed by a howl from one of the dogs. They all sprang up and ran towards the spot whence the sound came, just in time to see a panther bounding away with one of the dogs. A terrific yell of rage burst from every one, and each hastily threw something or other at the bold intruder. Pearson flung his knife and fork at it, having forgotten to drop those light weapons when he leaped up. The major hurled after it a heavy mass of firewood. Hardy and Hicks flung the huge marrow bones with which they happened to be engaged at the time. Tom Brown swung a large axe after it, and Wilkins, in desperation, shied his cap at it! But all missed their mark, and the panther would certainly have carried off his prize had not a very tall and powerfully-built Caffre, named Mafuta, darted at it an assegai, or long native spear, which, wounding it slightly, caused it to drop its prey.

The poor dog was severely hurt about the neck; it recovered, however, soon afterwards. The same night on which this oc-curred, one of the oxen was killed by a lion, but although all the people were more or less on the alert, the monarch of the woods escaped unpunished.

At an early hour next morning the train of wagons got into motion, and the hunters went out to their usual occupation.

# CHAPTER IV.

### Tom Sees Wonderful Sights, and at last has his Dreams Fulfilled.

Thus the travellers advanced day by day — sometimes in sunshine, sometimes in rain, now successful in hunting and now unsuccessful — until they reached the Zulu country and the banks of the river Umveloose.

Here they called a halt for a time, and began to hunt vigorously in all directions, aiming at every species of game. Our hero's first introduction to the river scenery was interesting, to himself at least, and singular. Having placed himself at the disposal of his friends to be appointed to whatever duty they pleased, he was sent off in the small boat belonging to the party with plenty of ammunition and provisions; Lieutenant Wilkins being his companion, and the tall Caffre, Mafuta, his guide and instructor in African warfare against the brute creation.

Between Tom Brown and this man Mafuta there had sprung up a species of friendship, which grew stronger the more they became acquainted with each other. Mafuta was an unusually honest, affectionate and straightforward Caffre, who had been much in the settlements, and could speak a little English. He first drew forth our hero's regard by nursing him with almost womanly tenderness during a three-days' severe illness at the beginning of the journey. Thereafter Tom gained his affection by repeated little acts of kindness, done in a quiet, offhand, careless way, as though he had pleasure in being kind, and did not care much whether the kindness were appreciated or not. He also excited his admiration by the imperturbable coolness and smiling good-humour with which he received every event in life; from the offer of an elephant steak to the charge of a black rhinoceros. Mafuta was also fond of Wilkins; but he worshipped Tom Brown.

On reaching the river the boat was launched on a part where there was nothing particularly striking to merit notice, so Tom said: "D'you know, Bob, I've taken a fancy to ramble alone for an hour along the banks of this river; will you, like a good fellow, get into the boat with Mafuta, and let me go along the banks on foot for a few miles. As your work will only be dropping down stream, you won't find it hard."

"By all means, Tom; a pleasant journey to you but see that you don't fall into the jaws of a lion or a crocodile!"

Our hero smiled as he waved his hand to his companions, and, turning away, was soon lost to sight among the bushes.

Now the fact was that Tom Brown, so far from being the unromantic creature that his name is erroneously supposed to imply, had such a superabundance of romance in his composition that he had, for some time past, longed to get away from his companions, and the noise and bustle of the wagon train, and go off alone into the solitudes of the great African wilderness, there to revel in the full enjoyment of the fact that he was in reality far far away from the haunts of civilised men; alone with primeval Nature!

The day happened to be delightful. Not too hot for walking, yet warm enough to incline one of Tom's temperament to throw open his vest and bare his broad bosom to any breeze that might chance to gambol through the forest. With characteristic nonchalance he pushed his wideawake off his forehead for the sake of coolness, and in so doing tilted it very much on one side, which gave him a somewhat rakish air. He carried his heavy double-barrelled gun on one of his broad shoulders with the butt behind him, and his right hand grasping the muzzle, while in his left he held a handkerchief, with which he occasionally wiped his heated brow. It was evident that Tom experienced the effects of the heat much, but he did not suffer from it. He perspired profusely, breathed heavily, and swaggered unwittingly, while a beaming smile played on his ruddy countenance, which told of peace with himself and with all mankind.

Not so, however, with brute kind, as became apparent after he had advanced about half a mile in a dreamy state down the banks of the quiet river, for, happening to observe something of a tawny yellow colour among the bushes, he brought his gun to the "present" with great precipitancy, cocked both barrels, and advanced with the utmost caution.

Up to this period he had not been successful in accomplishing his great wish — the shooting of a lion. Many a time had he heard the strong voices of the brutes, and once or twice had seen their forms dimly in the night sneaking round the bullocks wagons, but he had not yet managed to get a fair full view of the forest king, or a good shot at him. His heart now beat high with hope, for he believed that he was about to realise his ancient dream. Slowly, step by step, he advanced, avoiding the dense bushes, stepping lightly over the small ones, insinuating himself through holes and round stems, and conducting himself in a way that would have done credit to a North American Indian, until he gained a tree, close on the other side of which he knew the tawny object lay. With beating heart, but steady hand and frowning eye, he advanced another step and found — that the object was a yellow stone!

There was a sudden motion about Tom's jaws, as if he had gnashed his teeth, and a short gasp issued from his mouth, but that was all. The compressed steam was off; a smile wrinkled his visage immediately after, and quietly uncocking his gun he threw it over his shoulder and resumed his march.

On rounding a point a few minutes after, he was again arrested by a scene which, while it charmed, amazed him. Often had he observed the multitudes of living creatures with which the Creator has peopled that great continent, but never before had he beheld such a concentrated picture as was presented at that moment. Before him lay a wide stretch of the river, so wide, and apparently currentless, that it seemed like a calm lake, and so perfectly still that every object on and around it was faithfully mirrored on its depths — even the fleecy clouds that floated in the calm sky were repeated far down in the azure vault below.

Every part of this beautiful scene teemed with living creatures of every sort and size, from the huge alligators that lay like stranded logs upon the mud-banks, basking in the sun, to the tiny plover that waded in cheerful activity among the sedges. There were tall reeds in many places, and among these were thousands of cranes, herons, flamingoes, and other members of that long-necked and long-legged family; some engaged in solemnly searching for food, while others, already gorged, stood gravely on one leg, as if that position assisted digestion, and watched with quiet satisfaction the proceedings of their companions. The glassy surface of the mirror was covered in places with a countless host of geese, widgeons, teals and other water-fowl either gambolling about in sport, or sleeping away a recent surfeit, and thousands of other small birds and beasts swarmed about everywhere, giving a sort of faint indication of the inconceivable numbers of the smaller creatures which were there, though not visible to the observer. But Tom's interest was chiefly centred on the huge animals — the crocodiles and hippopotami — which sprawled or floated about.

Not far from the bush from behind which he gazed, two

large crocodiles lay basking on a mudbank — rugged and rough in the hide as two ancient trees — the one using the back of the other as a pillow. A little beyond these three hippopotami floated in the water, only the upper parts of their heads and rotund bodies being visible. These lay so motionless that they might have been mistaken for floating puncheons, and the observer would have thought them asleep, had he not noticed an occasional turn of the whites of their small eyes, and a slight puff of steam and water from their tightly compressed nostrils.

Truly it was a grand sight; one calculated to awaken in the most unthinking minds some thoughts about the infinite power of Him who made them all. Tom's mind did rise upwards for a little. Although not at that time very seriously inclined, he was, nevertheless, a man whose mind had been trained to think with reverence of his Creator. He was engaged in solemn contemplation of the scene before him, when a deep gurgling plunge almost under the bush at his feet aroused him. It was a hippopotamus which had been standing on the river-brink within six yards of the muzzle of his gun. Tom cocked and presented, but thinking that the position of the animal did not afford him a good chance of killing it, he waited, feeling sure, at all events, of securing one of the various huge creatures that were lying so near him.

It says much for Tom's powers of wood-craft that he managed to advance as near as he did to these animals without disturbing them. Few hunters could have done it; but it must be remembered that our hero, like all other heroes, was a man of unusual and astonishing parts!

While he hesitated for a few moments, undecided whether to fire at the crocodiles or the hippopotami, one of the latter suddenly uttered a prolonged snort or snore, and opened a mouth of such awful dimensions that Tom's head and shoulders would have easily found room in it. As he gazed into the dark red throat he felt that the wild fictions of untravelled men fell far short of the facts of actual life, in regard to grandeur and horribility, and it struck him that if the front half of a hippopotamus were sewed to the rear half of a crocodile there would be produced a monster incomparably more grand and horrible than the fiercest dragon St. George ever slew! While these ideas were passing quickly through his excited brain, the boat, which he had totally forgotten, came quietly round the bend of the river above him. But the sharp-eared and quick-eyed denizens of the wilderness were on the alert; it had scarcely shown its prow round the point of land, and the hippopotamus had not quite completed its lazy yawn, when the entire winged host rose with a rushing noise so thunderous, yet so soft and peculiar, that words cannot convey the idea of the sight and sound. At the same time, many grunts and snorts and heavy plunges told that sundry amphibious creatures had been disturbed, and were seeking safety in the clear stream.

Tom hesitated no longer. He aimed at the yawning hippopotamus and fired, hitting it on the skull, but at such an angle that the ball glanced off. If there was noise before, the riot and confusion now was indescribable! Water-fowl that had not moved at the first alarm now sprang in myriads from reeds and sedges, and darkened the very air. The two alligators just under Tom's nose spun their tails in the air with a whirl of awful energy that seemed quite incompatible with their sluggish nature, and rushed into the river. The hippopotami dived with a splash that covered the water around them with foam, and sent a wave of considerable size to the shore. The sudden burst of excitement, noise, splutter, and confusion was not less impressive than the previous calm had been, but Tom had not leisure to contemplate it, being himself involved in the whirl. Four shots from the boat told him that his companions were also engaged. One of the crocodiles re-appeared suddenly as if to have another look at Tom, who discharged his second barrel at it, sent a ball into its brain, and turned it over dead. He reloaded in great haste, and was in the act of capping when he heard a loud shout in the direction of the boat, and looking up, observed that Wilkins was standing in the bow gesticulating violently. He listened for a moment, but could not make out what he said.

"Hallo!" he cried, "shout louder; I don't hear you."

Again Wilkins shouted at the top of his voice, and waved his arms more frantically than before. Tom could not make out the words. He judged, however, that no man would put himself to such violent physical exertion without good reason, so he turned and looked cautiously around him. Presently he heard a crashing sound in the bushes, and a few moments afterwards observed three buffaloes tearing along the path in which he stood. It was these that Wilkins had seen from the boat when he attempted in vain to warn his friend. Tom jumped behind a bush, and as they passed tried to fire, but the foliage was so dense that he failed to get a good aim. Reserving his fire, therefore, he dashed after them at full speed. After running some distance the buffaloes stood still, and the nearest bull turned round and looked at Tom, who instantly sent a two ounce ball crashing into his shoulder. This turned them, and they all three made off at once, but the wounded one fell behind. Tom therefore stopped to reload, feeling pretty sure of him. Starting off in pursuit, he gained on the wounded animal at every stride, and was about to fire again, when his limbs were for a moment paralysed, and his heart was made almost to stand still at the sight of three full-grown lions which sprang at the unfortunate brute from a neighbouring thicket. They had no doubt gone there to rest for the day, but the sight of a lame and bleeding buffalo was a temptation too strong for them. The lions did not leap upon him, but, seizing him with their teeth and claws, stood on their hind legs and tried to tear him down with terrible ferocity.

Our hero, who, as we have said, was for a few moments bereft of the power of action, could do nothing but stand and gaze in amazement. All the dreams of his youth and manhood were as nothing to this! The poor buffalo fought nobly, but it had no chance against such odds, and would certainly have been torn to pieces and devoured had not Tom recovered his self-possession in a few minutes. Creeping up to within thirty yards he fired at one of the lions with such good aim that it fell dead almost on the spot, having time only to turn and seize a bush savagely with its teeth ere it died. The second barrel was discharged, but not with the same effect. Another of the lions was wounded, and sprang into the bushes with an angry roar. The third merely lifted his head, looked at Tom for a moment as if with indignant surprise, and then went on tearing at the carcass as hard as ever.

With a feeling of thankfulness that this particular king of the forest had treated him so contemptuously, Tom slunk behind a tree and recharged his gun, after which he advanced cautiously and sent a ball crashing through the lion's shoulder. It *ought* to have killed him, he thought, but it did not, for he made off as fast as possible, just as Wilkins and Mafuta arrived, panting, on the scene of action.

"What a magnificent fellow!" exclaimed Wilkins going up to the dead lion. "Bravissimo, Tom, you've done it at last."

"Done *it*!" cried Tom, as he loaded hastily, "why, I've all but done *three*. Follow up the trail, man, as fast as you can. I'll overtake you in no time!"

Wilkins did not wait for more, but dashed into the thicket after Mafuta, who had preceded him.

Tom was quickly on their heels, and they had not gone far when one of the wounded lions was found lying on the ground quite dead. The other was not overtaken, but, as Wilkins said, two lions, a buffalo, and a hippopotamus, which latter he had shot from the boat, was not a bad beginning!

That night they encamped under the shelter of a spreading tree, and as they reclined at full length between two fires, which were kindled to keep off the wild beasts, enjoying a pipe after having feasted luxuriously on hippopotamus steaks and marrow bones, Tom Brown remarked: "Well, my dream has been realised at last, and, upon my word, I have not been disappointed."

# CHAPTER V.

*More about Lions!*

As we have now introduced our readers to the lion, we think it but right to say something about his aspect and character, as given by some of our best authorities.

Dr. Livingstone, that greatest of African travellers, seems to be of opinion that untravelled men are prone to overrate the lion, both as to his appearance and courage. From him we learn that when a lion is met with in the day-time — a circumstance by no means uncommon in Africa — the traveller will be disappointed with the appearance of the animal which they had been accustomed to hear styled "noble" and "majestic"; that it is somewhat larger than the largest-sized dog, partakes very strongly of the canine features, and does not much resemble our usual drawings of lions, which he condemns as bearing too strong a resemblance to "old women's faces in nightcaps." The Doctor also talks slightingly of its roar, and says that having made particular inquiry as to the opinions of European travellers who have heard the roar of the lion and that of the ostrich, he found they invariably admitted that they could not detect any difference between the two when the animals were at a distance.

Now, really, although we are bound to admit that the Doctor's opinion is of great weight, we cannot, without a humble protest, allow ourselves to be thus ruthlessly stripped of all our romantic notions in regard to the "king of beasts"! We suspect that the Doctor, disgusted with the "twaddle" that has undoubtedly been talked in all ages about the "magnanimity" of the "noble" lion and his "terrific aspect," has been led unintentionally to underrate him. In this land we have opportunities of seeing and hearing the lion in his captive state; and we think that most readers will sympathise with us when we say that even in a cage he has at least a very grand and noble *aspect*; and that, when about to be fed, his intermittent growls and small roars, so to speak, have something very awful and impressive, which nothing like the bellowing of a bull can at all equal. To say that the roar of the ostrich is equal to that of the lion is no argument at all; it does not degrade the latter, it merely exalts the former. And further, in regard to aspect, the illustrations in Dr. Livingstone's own most interesting work go far to prove that the lion is magnificent in appearance.

Thus much we dare venture to say, because on these points we, with all men, are in a position to form a judgment for ourselves. We, however, readily believe the great traveller when he tells us that nothing he ever heard of the lion led him to ascribe to it a noble *character*, and that it possesses none of the nobility of the Newfoundland or St. Bernard Dogs. The courage of the lion, although not greater than that of most large and powerful animals, is, without doubt, quite sufficient! But he fortunately possesses a wholesome dread of man, else would he certainly long ere now have become king of Africa as well as of beasts. When encountered in the day-time, he usually stands a second or two gazing, then turns slowly round and walks leisurely away for a dozen paces or so, looking over his shoulder as he goes. Soon he begins to trot, and, when he thinks himself out of sight, bounds off like a greyhound. As a rule, there is not the smallest danger of a lion attacking man by day, if he be not molested, except when he happens to have a wife and young family with him. Then, indeed, his bravery will induce him to face almost any danger. If a man happens to pass to windward of a lion and lioness with cubs, both parents will rush at him, but instances of this kind ere of rare occurrence.

It would seem that light of any kind has a tendency to scare away lions. Bright moonlight is a safeguard against them, as well as daylight. So well is this understood, that on moonlight nights it is not thought necessary to tie up the oxen, which are left loose by the wagons, while on dark rainy nights it is deemed absolutely necessary to tether them, because if a lion chanced to be in the vicinity, he would be almost sure to attack, and perhaps kill, an ox, notwithstanding the vigilance of guards and the light of the camp-fires. He always approaches stealthily, like the cat, except when wounded; but anything having the appearance of a trap will induce him to refrain from making the last fatal spring. This is a peculiarity of the whole feline species. It has been found in India that when a hunter pickets a goat on a plain as a bait, a tiger has whipped it off so quickly by a stroke of his paw that it was impossible to take aim. To obviate this difficulty a small pit is dug, in the bottom of which the goat is picketed, with a small stone tied in its ear to make it cry the whole night. When the suspicious tiger sees the appearance of a trap he walks round and round the pit, thus giving the hunter in ambush a fair shot.

When a hungry lion is watching for prey, the sight of any animal will make him commence stalking it. On one occasion a man was very busy stalking a rhinoceros, when, happening to glance behind him, he found to his consternation that a lion was *stalking him*! he escaped by springing up a tree.

The strength of the lion is tremendous, owing to the immense mass of muscle around its jaws, shoulders, and forearms. What one hears, however, of his sometimes seizing an ox or a horse in his mouth and running away with it, as a cat does with a mouse, and even leaping hedges, etc., is nonsense. Dr. Livingstone says that most of the feats of strength he has seen per-formed by lions consisted, not in carrying, but dragging or trailing the carcass along the ground.

He usually seizes his prey by the flank near the hind leg, or by the throat below the jaw. He has his particular likings and tit-bits, and is very expert in carving out the parts of an animal that please him best. An eland may be sometimes disembowelled by a lion so completely that he scarcely seems cut up at all, and the bowels and fatty parts of the interior form a full meal for the lion, however large or hungry he may be. His pert little follower the jackal usually goes after him, sniffing about and waiting for a share, and is sometimes punished for his impudent familiarity with a stroke of the lion's paw, which of course kills him.

Lions are never seen in herds, but sometimes six or eight — probably one family — are seen hunting together. Much has been said and written about the courage of the lion, and his ability to attack and kill any other animal. His powers in this respect have been overrated. It is questionable if a single lion ever attacks a full-grown buffalo. When he assails a calf, the cow will rush upon him, and one toss from her horns is sufficient to kill him. The amount of roaring usually heard at night, when a buffalo is killed, seems to indicate that more than one lion has been engaged in the fight. They never attack any elephants, except the calves. "Every living thing," writes Livingstone, "retires before the lordly elephant, yet a full-grown one would be an easier prey to the lion than a rhinoceros. The lion rushes off at the mere sight of this latter beast!"

When a lion grows too old to hunt game, he frequently retires to spend the decline of life in the suburbs of a native vil-lage, where he is well content to live by killing goats. A woman or a child happening to go out at night sometimes falls a prey also. Being unable, of course, to alter this style of life, when once he is reduced to it, he becomes habitually what is styled a "man-eater," and from this circumstance has arisen the idea that when a lion has once tasted human flesh he prefers it to any other. In reality a "man-eater" is an old fellow who cannot manage to get anything else to eat, and who might perhaps be more appropriately styled a woman and child eater! When extreme old age comes upon him in the remote deserts, far from human habitations, he is constrained to appease the cravings of hunger with mice! The African lion is of a tawny colour, like that of some mastiffs. The mane in the male is large, and gives the idea of great power. In some the ends of the hair are black, and these go by the name of black-maned lions, but, as a whole, all of them look of a tawny yellow colour.

Having said thus much about his general character and appearance, we shall resume the thread of our story, and show how the lions behaved to Tom Brown and his friends the very night after the event narrated in the last chapter.

The hunters had got back to the wagons, and were about to turn in for the night, in order to recruit for the work of the following day, when the sky became overcast, and gave every indication of a coming storm. A buffalo bull had been shot by Pearson an hour before the arrival of our hero and his companions, and the Caffres were busily engaged on his carcass. A fire had been lighted, the animal cut up, and part of him roasted, and the natives alternately ate a lump of roasted flesh and an equal quantity of the inside raw! When the sky began to darken, however, they desisted for a time, and set about making preparations for the coming storm.

It burst upon them ere long with awful fury and grandeur, the elements warring with incredible vehemence. Rain fell in such floods that it was scarcely possible to keep the fires burning, and the night was so pitchy dark that the hand could scarcely be seen when held close to the eyes. To add to the horror of the scene, crashing peals of thunder appeared to rend the sky, and these were preceded by flashes of lightning so vivid that each left the travellers with the impression of being stone-blind.

After an hour or two the storm passed by, leaving them drenched to the skin. However, the fires were stirred up, and things made as comfortable as circumstances would admit of.

Just a little before daybreak they were all wakened by the bellowing of the oxen and the barking of dogs.

"Something there," muttered Hicks, leaping up and seizing his gun.

The major, Tom Brown, Wilkins, Pearson, and the others were immediately on their feet and wide awake. There was just light enough to distinguish objects dimly when close at hand; but the surrounding woods resembled a wall of impenetrable darkness. Close to the wagon in which our hero lay the natives had erected a temporary hut of grass, about six feet high. On the top of this he saw a dark form, which, by the sound of his voice, he recognised to be that of a native named Jumbo, who was more noted for good nature and drollery than for courage. He was shouting lustily for a percussion-cap. Tom sprang on the top of the hut and supplied him with several caps, at the same time exclaiming: —

"Hallo! Jumbo, don't make such a row. You'll scare everything away."

"Ho! Me wish um could," said Jumbo, his teeth chattering in his head with fear as he listened to the dying groans of a poor ox, and heard the lions growling and roaring beside him. They were not more than fourteen yards off, but so dark was the night that they could not be seen. The ox, however, which was a black one, was faintly distinguishable; Tom Brown therefore aimed, as near as he could guess, about a foot above him and fired. No result followed. He had evidently missed. While he was re-loading, the major and Wilkins rushed forward and leaped on the hut, exclaiming eagerly, "Where are they? have you hit?" Immediately afterwards, Pearson, Brand, Ogilvie, and Anson rushed up and attempted to clamber on the hut.

"No room here," cried the major, resisting them, "quite full outside — inside not safe!"

"But there's no room on the wagon," pleaded Pearson; "the niggers are clustering on it like monkeys."

"Can't help it," replied the major, "there's not an inch of —"

Here a tremendous roar interrupted him, and a loud report followed, as Jumbo and Wilkins, having caught sight of "something" near the carcass, fired simultaneously. Pearson and his companions in trouble vanished like smoke, while the major, failing to see anything, fired in the direction of the lions on chance. Tom also fired at what he felt convinced was the head of a lioness. Still the animals appeared to be unhurt and indifferent! The sportsmen were busy loading when Tom became aware, for one instant, that something was moving in the air. Next moment he was knocked backwards off the hut, head over heels, several times, having been struck full in the chest by a lion's head. Half inclined to believe that he was killed he scrambled to his feet, still holding fast to his gun, however, like a true hunter, and rushed towards the wagon, where he found all the Caffres who could not get inside sticking on the outside, as Pearson had said, like mon-keys. There was literally no room for more, but Tom cared not for that. He seized legs, arms, and hair indiscriminately, and in another moment was on the top of the living mass. He had leaped very smartly to this point of vantage, nevertheless he found Jumbo there before him, chattering worse than ever! The major and and Wilkins came up breathless next moment, clam-bered halfway up, slipped, and fell to the ground with a united roar; but making a second attempt, they succeeded in getting up. Wilkins at once presented in the direction of the lions and again fired. Whether any of them fell is a matter of dispute, but certain it is that Wilkins fell, for the recoil of the gun knocked him back, his footing being insecure, and he went down on the top of a tent which had been pitched on the other side of the wagon, and broke the pole of it. After this several more shots were fired, apparently without success. While they were reloading a lion leaped on a goat, which was tethered to the grass-hut, and carried it away before any one could fire. Not daring to descend from their places of security, there the whole party sat in the cold during the remainder of that night, listening to the growling of the lions as they feasted on their prey. It was not till grey dawn appeared that the enemy beat a retreat, and allowed the shivering travellers to get once more between the blankets. They had not lain long, however, when a double shot aroused them all, and they rushed out to find that Mafuta had killed a lioness! She was a splendid creature, and had succumbed to a bullet sent through her ribs. It was found on examination that another ball had hit her just behind the head, and travelling along the spine, had stuck near the root of the tail.

"Me no hab fire at head," said Mafuta, with a disappointed look. "Me hit him in ribs wid wan bar'l, an' miss him wid tother."

"What is that you say?" cried Tom Brown examining the bullet-hole; "ha! I claim that lioness, because I fired at her head last night, and there you have the bullet-hole."

"Cut out the ball and see," said Hicks, drawing his knife.

When the ball was extracted it was indeed found to have been fired from Tom's gun, so, according to sporting law in that region, which ordains that he who first draws blood claims the game, the lioness was adjudged to belong to Tom.

Our hero returned to his blankets once more, congratulating himself not a little on his good fortune, when his attention was arrested by two shots in succession at no great distance. Seizing his gun he ran to the place expecting to find that more game had been slain, but he only found Hardy standing over one of the oxen which was breathing its last. The lions had driven it mad with terror during the night, and the trader had been obliged to shoot it. This was a great misfortune, for it was about the best ox in the train.

# CHAPTER VI.

### *Gives a Few Hints to Would-be Hunters, and a Friend in Need is Introduced.*

In describing the principal incidents of a long journey, it is impossible to avoid crowding them together, so as to give a somewhat false impression of the expedition as a whole. The reader must not suppose that our hunters were perpetually engaged in fierce and deadly conflict with wild beasts and furious elements! Although travelling in Africa involves a good deal more of this than is to be experienced in most other parts of the world, it is not without its periods of calm and repose. Neither must it be imagined that the hunters — whom hitherto we have unavoidably exhibited in the light of men incapable of being overcome either by fatigues or alarms — were always in robust health, ready at any moment to leap into the grasp of a lion or the jaws of a crocodile. Their life, on the whole, was checkered. Sometimes health prevailed in the camp, and all went on well and heartily; so that they felt disposed to regard wagon-travelling — in the words of a writer of great experience — as a prolonged system of picnicking, excellent for the health, and agreeable to those who are not over-fastidious about trifles, and who delight in being in the open air. At other times, especially when passing through unhealthy regions, some of their number were brought very low by severe illness, and others — even the strongest — suffered from the depressing influence of a deadly climate. But they were all men of true pluck, who persevered through heat and cold, health and sickness, until, in two instances, death terminated their career.

It may not be out of place here to make a few remarks for the benefit of those ardent spirits who feel desperately heroic and emulative when reading at their own firesides, and who are tempted by descriptions of adventure to set their hearts on going forth to "do and dare," as others have done and dared before them! All men are not heroes, and in many countries men may become average hunters without being particularly heroic. In Norway, for instance, and in North America, any man of ordinary courage may become a Nimrod; and even heroes will have opportunities afforded them of facing dangers of a sufficiently appalling nature, if they choose to throw themselves in their way; but in Africa a man must be *really* a hero if he would come off scatheless and with credit. We have proved this to some extent already, and more proof is yet to come. The dangers that one encounters in hunting there are not only very great and sufficiently numerous, but they are absolutely unavoidable. The writer before quoted says on this point: "A young sportsman, no matter how great among foxes, pheasants, and hounds, would do well to pause before resolving to brave fever for the excitement of risking the terrific charge of the elephant. The step of that enormous brute when charging the hunter, though apparently not quick, is so long that the pace equals the speed of a good horse at a canter. Its trumpeting or screaming when infuriated is more like what the shriek of a French steam-whistle would be to a man standing on the dangerous part of a railroad than any other earthly sound. A horse unused to it will sometimes stand shivering instead of taking his rider out of danger. It has happened often that the poor animal's legs do their duty so badly that he falls and exposes his rider to be trodden into a mummy; or losing his presence of mind, the rider may allow the horse to dash under a tree, and crack his cranium against a branch. As one charge of an elephant has often been enough to make embryo hunters bid a final adieu to the chase, incipient Nimrods would do well to try their nerves by standing on railways till the engines are within a few yards of them, before going to Africa!"

Begging pardon for this digression, we return to our tale. While our sportsmen were advancing in company with the bullock-wagons one evening, at the close of a long and trying day, in which they had suffered a good deal from want of good water, they fell in with another party travelling in the opposite direction, and found that they belonged to the train of a missionary who had been on an expedition into the interior.

They gladly availed themselves of the opportunity thus afforded of encamping with a countryman, and called a halt for the night at a spot where a desert well existed.

As they sat round the fire that night, the missionary gave them some interesting and useful information about the country and the habits of the animals, as well as the condition of the natives.

"Those who inhabit this region," said he, "have always been very friendly to us, and listen attentively to instruction conveyed to them in their own tongue. It is, however, difficult to give an idea to an Englishman of the little effect produced by our teaching, because no one can realise the degradation to which their minds have sunk by centuries of barbarism and hard struggling for the necessaries of life. Like most other savages, they listen with respect and attention to our talk; but when we kneel down and address an unseen Being, the position and the act often appear to them so ridiculous, that they cannot refrain from bursting into uncontrollable laughter. After a short time, however, they get over this tendency. I was once present when a brother missionary attempted to sing in the midst of a wild heathen tribe of natives who had no music in their composition, and the effect on the risible faculties of the audience was such that the tears actually ran down their cheeks."

"Surely, if this be so," said Tom Brown, "it is scarcely worth your while to incur so much labour, expense, and hardship for the sake of results so trifling."

"I have not spoken of results, but of beginnings," replied the missionary. "Where our efforts have been long-continued we have, through God's blessing, been successful, I sincerely believe, in bringing souls to the Saviour. Of the effects of long-continued instruction there can be no reasonable doubt, and a mere nominal belief has never been considered by any body of missionaries as a sufficient proof of conversion. True, our progress has been slow, and our difficulties have been great; but let me ask, my dear sir, has the slowness of your own journey to this point, and its great difficulty, damped your ardour or induced you to think it scarcely worth your while to go on?"

"Certainly not," replied Tom; "I don't mean to give in yet. I confess that our 'bag' is not at present very large — nothing compared to what some sportsmen have had; but then if we persevere for a few months we are almost certain to succeed, whereas in your case the labour of many years seems to have been very much in vain."

"Not in vain," answered the other, "our influence has been powerfully felt, although the results are not obviously clear to every one who casts a mere passing glance at us and our field of labour. But you speak of persevering labour in hunting as being almost certain of success, whereas we missionaries are *absolutely* certain of it, because the Word, which cannot err, tells us that our labour is not in vain in the Lord, and, besides, even though we had no results at all to point to, we have the command, from which, even if we would, we cannot escape, 'Go ye into all the world, and preach the gospel to every creature.'"

"Well, sir," said the major, with the air of a man who highly approves of the philanthropic efforts of all men, so long as they do not interfere with the even tenor of his own way, "I am sure that your disinterested labours merit the gratitude of all good men, and I heartily wish you success. In the course of your remarks to-night you have happened to mention that peculiar bird the ostrich. May I ask if you have seen many of late?"

The missionary smiled at this very obvious attempt to change the subject of conversation, but readily fell in with the major's humour, and replied —

"Oh yes, you will find plenty of them in the course of a few days, if you hold on the course you are going."

"Is it true that he goes at the pace of a railway locomotive?" asked Wilkins.

"It is not possible," replied the missionary, laughing, "to give a direct answer to that question, inasmuch as the speed of the locomotive varies."

"Well, say thirty miles an hour," said Wilkins.

"His pace is not far short of that," answered the other. "When walking, his step is about twenty-six inches long, but when terrified and forced to run, his stride is from twelve to four-teen feet in length. Once I had a pretty fair opportunity of counting his rate of speed with a stop-watch, and found that there were about thirty steps in ten seconds; this, taking his average stride at twelve feet, gives a speed of twenty-six miles an hour. Generally speaking, one's eye can no more follow the legs than it can the spokes of a carriage wheel in rapid motion."

"I do hope we may succeed in falling in with one," observed the major.

"If you do there is not much chance of your shooting it," said the missionary.

"Why not?"

"Because he is so difficult to approach. Usually he feeds on some open spot where no one can approach him without being detected by his wary eye. However, you have this in your favour, that his stupidity is superior to his extreme caution. If a wagon should chance to move along far to windward of him, he evidently thinks it is trying to circumvent him, for instead of making off to leeward, as he might easily do, he rushes up to windward with the intention of passing *ahead* of the wagon, and sometimes passes so near the front oxen that one may get a shot at the silly thing. I have seen this stupidity of his taken advantage of when he was feeding in a valley open at both ends. A number of men would commence running as if to cut off his retreat from the end through which the wind came, and although he had the whole country hundreds of miles before him by going to the other end, he rushed madly on to get past the men, and so was speared, for it is one of his peculiarities that he never swerves from the course he has once adopted, but rushes wildly and blindly forward, anxious only to increase his speed. Sometimes a horseman may succeed in killing him by cutting across his undeviating course. It is interesting to notice a resemblance between this huge bird and our English wild duck or plover. I have several times seen newly-hatched young in charge of a cock-ostrich who made a very good attempt at appearing lame in order to draw off the attention of pursuers. The young squat down and remain immoveable, when too small to run far, but they attain a wonderful degree of speed when about the size of common fowls. It requires the utmost address of the bushmen, creeping for miles on their stomach, to stalk them successfully; yet the quantity of feathers collected annually shows that the numbers slain must be considerable, as each bird has only a few feathers in the wings and tail."

"Well," observed the major, shaking the ashes out of his pipe, "your account of the bird makes me hope that we shall fall in with him before our expedition is over."

"Do you mean to be out long?"

"As long as we can manage, which will be a considerable time," answered the major, "because we are well supplied with everything, except, I regret to say, medicine. The fact is that none of us thought much about that, for we have always been in such a robust state of health that we have scarce believed in the possibility of our being knocked down; but the first few weeks of our journey hither taught some of us a lesson when too late."

"Ah, we are often taught lessons when too late," said the missionary; "however, it is not too late on this occasion, for I am happy to say that I can supply you with all the physic you require."

The major expressed much gratification on hearing this, and indeed he felt it, for the country into which they were about to penetrate was said to be rather unhealthy.

"You are very kind, sir," he said; "my companions and I shall feel deeply indebted to you for this opportune assistance."

"Are you quite sure," asked the missionary pointedly, "that you are supplied with everything else that you require?"

"I think so," replied the major. "Let me see — yes, I don't know that we need anything more, now that you have so kindly offered to supply us with physic, which I had always held, up to the period of my residence in Africa, was fit only to be thrown to the dog."

The missionary looked earnestly in the major's face, and said —

"Excuse me, sir, have you got a Bible?"

"Well — a—really, my dear sir," he replied, somewhat confusedly, "I must confess that I have not. The fact is, that it is somewhat inconvenient to carry books in such regions, and I did not think of bringing a Bible. Perhaps some one of our party may have one, however."

None of the party replied to the major's look except Tom

Brown, who quietly said —

"There is one, I believe, in the bottom of my trunk; one of my sisters told me she put it there, but I cannot say positively that I have seen it."

"Will you accept of one?" said the missionary, rising; "we start at an early hour in the morning, and before going I would like to remind you, gentlemen, that eternity is near — nearer perchance than we suppose to some of us, and that medicine is required for the soul even more than for the body. Jesus Christ, the great Physician, will teach you how to use it, if you will seek advice from himself. I feel assured that you will not take this parting word ill. Good night, gentlemen. I will give the drugs to your guide before leaving, and pray that God may prosper you in your way and give you success."

There was a long silence round the camp-fire after the missionary had left. When night closed in, and the sportsmen had retired to rest, the minds of most of them dwelt somewhat seriously on the great truth which he had stated — that medicine is needed not only for the body but the soul.

# CHAPTER VII.

### *Describes River Hunting.*

"Well, major, what are your orders for the day?" asked Tom Brown one fine morning after breakfast, while they were enjoying their usual pipe under the shade of a large umbrageous tree.

"You'd better try the river that we have just come to," said the major.

"Do you think me amphibious, that you should always assign me that work?" asked Tom.

"Not exactly, Tom, but I know you are fond of telling fibs, and perhaps the amphibious animals may afford you some scope in that way. At all events they are capable of such astonishing feats that if you merely relate the truth about them you will be sure to get credit in England for telling fibs – like poor Mungo Park, who was laughed at all his life for a notorious drawer of the long-bow, although there never was a more truthful man."

"People won't judge *us* so harshly, major," said Wilkins; "for so many African travellers have corroborated Mungo Park's stories that the truth is pretty well known and believed by people of average education. But pray is it your lordship's pleasure that I should accompany Tom? You know he cannot take care of himself, and no one of the party can act so powerfully as a check on his inveterate propensity to inordinate smoking as myself."

"You must have studied Johnson's dictionary very closely in your boyhood," said Tom, puffing a prolonged cloud as a termination to the sentence.

"But, major, if you do condemn me to his company, please let us have Mafuta again, for Wilkins and I are like two uncongenial stones, and he acts as lime to keep us together."

"Don't you think that Hicks had better be consulted before we make arrangements?" suggested Pearson.

"Hear, hear," cried Ogilvie; "and I should like to know what is to be done with Brand and Anson, for they are both very much down with fever of some sort this morning."

"Leave Jumbo with them," said Tom Brown; "he's better at nursing than hunting. By the way, was it not he who nursed the native that died last night in the kraal?"

"It was, and they say he killed the poor nigger by careless treatment," said Pearson.

"What nigger do you refer to?" asked Ogilvie.

"The one who died — but, I forgot, you were out after that hyena when it happened, and so I suppose have not heard of it," said Pearson. "We had a funeral in the village over there last night, and they say that our fellow Jumbo, who it seems was once a friend of the sick man, offered to sit up with him last night. There is a rumour that he was an enemy of Jumbo's, and that our cowardly scoundrel made this offer in order to have an opportunity of killing him in a quiet way. Hicks even goes the length of saying he is sure that Jumbo killed him, for when he saw the sick man last he was under the impression what he had got the turn, and gave him a powder that would have been certain to cure —"

"Or kill," interrupted Tom Brown; "I've no faith in Hicks's skill as a practitioner."

"Of course not," said Wilkins, "proverbial philosophy asserts and requires that doctors should disagree."

"Be that as it may," continued Pearson, "the native did die and was buried, so that's an end of him, and yonder sits Jumbo eating his breakfast at the camp-fire as if he had done a most virtuous action. The fact is, I don't believe the reports. I cannot believe that poor Jumbo, coward though he is, would be guilty of such an act."

"Perhaps not," said the major, rising, "but there's no possibility of settling the question now, and here comes Hicks, so I'll go and make arrangements with him about the day's proceedings."

"They have a primitive mode of conducting funerals here," said Tom Brown when the major had left. "I happened to be up at the kraal currying favour with the chief man, for he has the power of bothering us a good deal if he chooses, and I observed what they did with this same dead man. I saw that he was very low as I passed the hut where he lay, and stopped to look on. His breath was very short, and presently he fell into what either might have been a profound sleep, or a swoon, or death; I could not be quite sure which, not being used to black fellows. I would have examined the poor man, but the friends kicked up a great row and shoved me off. Before the breath could have been well out of his body, they hoisted him up and carried him away to burial. I followed out of mere curiosity, and found that the lazy rascals had shoved the body into an ant-eater's hole in order to save the trouble of digging a grave."

While Tom and his friends were thus conversing over their pipes, their attention was attracted by a peculiar cry or howl of terror, such as they had never heard from any animal of those regions. Starting up they instinctively grasped their guns and looked about them. The utterer of the cry was soon obvious in the person of Jumbo, who had leaped up suddenly — overturning his breakfast in the act — and stood gazing before him with his eyes starting out of their sockets, his teeth rattling together like a pair of castanets, his limbs quivering, and in fact his whole person displaying symptoms of the most abject terror of which the human frame is capable.

The major and Hicks, who stood not far from him, were both unusually pale in the face, as they gazed motionless before them.

The fixedness of their looks directed the eyes of Tom Brown and his comrades towards a neighbouring thicket, where they beheld an object that was well calculated to inspire dread. It appeared to be a living skeleton covered with a black skin of the most ghastly appearance, and came staggering towards them like a drunken man. As it drew nearer Jumbo's limbs trembled more and more violently and his face became of a leaden blue colour. At last he became desperate, turned round, dashed right through the embers of the fire, and fled wildly from the spot with a howl that ended in a shriek of terror.

"No wonder he's terrified," observed Tom Brown to his alarmed comrades; "I felt more than half certain the nigger was not dead last night, and now it is beyond question that they had buried him alive. Jumbo evidently thinks it's his ghost!"

"*Won't* he give his friend a fright?" said Wilkins, on observing that the poor man went staggering on in the direction of the kraal.

"He will," said Hicks, laughing; "but they'll make up for their haste by taking good care of him now. I declare I thought for a moment or two that it was a real ghost! Come now, gentlemen, if you want good sport you've got the chance before you to-day. The last party that passed this way left an old boat on the river. I dare say it won't be very leaky. Some of you had better take it and go after the 'potimusses. There's plenty of buffalo and elephants in this region also, and the natives are anxious to have a dash at them along with you. Divide yourselves as you choose, and I'll go up to make arrangements with the old chief."

In accordance with the trader's advice the party was divided.

Tom Brown, Wilkins, and Mafuta, as on a former occasion, determined to stick together and take to the boat. The others, under the major, went with Hicks and the natives after elephants.

"Another capital stream," remarked Tom to his companion as they emerged from the bushes on the banks of a broad river, the surface of which was dotted here and there with log-like hippopotami, some of which were floating quietly, while others plunged about in the water.

"Capital!" exclaimed Wilkins, "now for the boat! According to directions we must walk upstream till we find it."

As they advanced, they came suddenly on one of the largest crocodiles they had yet seen. It was lying sound asleep on a mudbank, not dreaming, doubtless, of the daring bipeds who were about to disturb its repose.

"Hallo!" exclaimed Wilkins, cocking and levelling his gun, "what a splendid chance!"

It was indeed a splendid chance, for the brute was twenty feet long at least; the rugged knobs of its thick hide showed here and there through a coat of mud with which it was covered, and its partially open jaws displayed a row of teeth that might have made the lion himself shrink. The mud had partially dried in the sun, so that the monster, as it lay sprawling, might have been mistaken for a dead carcass, had not a gentle motion about the soft parts of his body given evidence of life.

Before Wilkins could pull the trigger, Mafuta seized him by the arm with a powerful grip.

"Hold on!" he cried with a look of intense anxiety, "what you go do? Fright all de 'potimus away for dis yer crackodl. Oh fy! go away."

"That's true, Bob," said Tom Brown, who, although he had prepared to fire in case of need, intended to have allowed his friend to take the first shot; "'twould be a pity to lose our chance of a sea-cow, which is good for food, for the sake of a monster which at the best could only give us a fine specimen-head for a museum, for his entire body is too big to haul about through the country after us."

Well, be it so, said Wilkins, somewhat disappointed, "but I'm determined to kick him up anyhow."

Saying this he advanced towards the brute, but again the powerful hand of Mafuta seized him.

"What you do? want git kill altogidder? You is a fool! (the black had lost temper a little). Him got nuff strong in hims tail to crack off de legs of 'oo like stem-pipes. Yis, kom back?"

Wilkins felt a strong tendency to rebel, and the Caffre remonstrated in so loud a voice that the crocodile awoke with a start, and immediately convinced the obstinate hunter that he had at least been saved broken bones by Mafuta, for he never in his life before had seen anything like the terrific whirl that he gave his tail, as he dashed into the water some fifteen yards ahead. Almost immediately afterwards he turned round, and there, floating like a log on the stream, took a cool survey of the disturbers of his morning's repose!

"It's hard to refuse such an impudent invitation to do one's worst," said Wilkins, again raising his gun.

"No, you mustn't," cried Tom Brown, grasping his friend's arm; "come along, I see the bow of the boat among the rushes not far ahead of us, and yonder is a hippopotamus, or sea-cow as they call it here, waiting to be shot."

Without further delay they embarked in the boat, which, though small, was found to be sufficiently tight, and rowed off towards the spot where the hippopotamus had been seen. Presently his blunt ungainly head rose within ten feet of them. Wilkins got such a start that he tripped over one of the thwarts in trying to take aim, and nearly upset the boat. He recovered himself, however, in a moment, and fired — sending a ball into the brute which just touched the brain and stunned it. He then fired his second barrel, and while he was loading Tom put two more balls into it. It proved hard to kill, however, for they fired alternately, and put sixteen bullets — seven to the pound — into different parts of its head before they succeeded in killing it.

They towed their prize to the shore, intending to land and secure it, when a calf hippopotamus shoved its blunt nose out of the water close at hand, gazed stupidly at them and snorted. Tom at once shot it in the head, and it commenced to bellow lustily. Instantly the mother's head cleft the surface of the water as she came up to the rescue and rushed at the boat, the gunwale of which she seized in her mouth and pulled it under.

"Quick!" shouted Tom, as he fired his second barrel into her ear.

Wilkins did not require to be urged, as the water was flowing into the boat like a deluge. He delivered both shots into her almost simultaneously, and induced her to let go! Another shot from Tom in the back of her neck entered the spine and killed her.

By this time a large band of natives had collected, and were gazing eagerly on the proceedings. They had come down from the kraal to enjoy the sport and get some of the meat, of which they are particularly fond. They were not disappointed in their expectations, for the hippopotami were very numerous in that place, and the sportsmen shot well. Four other animals fell before their deadly guns before another hour had passed, and as the bay was shallow the natives waded in to drag them ashore.

This was a very amusing scene, because crocodiles were so numerous that it was only possible for them to accomplish the work safely by entering the water together in large numbers, with inconceivable noise, yelling and splashing, in order to scare them away. They would not have ventured in singly, or in small numbers, on any account whatever; but on the present occasion, being numerous, they were very courageous, and joining hands, so as to form a line from the shore to the floating animals, soon dragged them out.

As the carcasses belonged to Hicks the trader, these black fellows knew well enough that they were not at liberty to do with them as they pleased, so they waited as patiently as they could for the glorious feast which they fondly hoped was in store for them.

When the sportsmen at last landed to look after their game, they found four fine sea-cows and the calf drawn up on the banks, side by side, with upwards of a hundred Caffres gazing at them longingly! Nothing could be more courteous than the behaviour of these savages when Mafuta cut off such portions as his party required; but no sooner was the remainder of the spoil handed over to them than there ensued a scene of indescribable confusion. They rushed at the carcasses like vultures, with assegais, knives, sticks, and axes, hallooing, bellowing, shoving, and fighting, in a manner that would have done credit to the wildest of the wild beasts by which they were surrounded! Yet there was a distinct sense of justice among them. It was indeed a desperate fight to obtain possession, but no one attempted to dispossess another of what he had been fortunate enough to secure. The strongest savages got at the carcasses first, and cut off large lumps, which they hurled to their friends outside the struggling circle. These caught the meat thus thrown, and ran with it, each to a separate heap, on which he deposited his piece and left it in perfect security.

In order to introduce a little more fair play, however, for the benefit of the weaker brethren, Mafuta dashed in among them with a terrible sjambok, or whip, of rhinoceros hide, which he laid about him with wonderful effect. In a very short time the whole of the meat was disposed of, not a scrap being left large enough to satisfy the cravings of the smallest conceivable crocodile that ever dwelt in that river!

The effects of this upon the native mind was immediate and satisfactory. That night the sportsmen received from the kraal large and gratifying gifts of eggs, bread, rice, beer, pumpkins, and all the produce of the land.

But we must not forestall. Before these dainties were enjoyed that night the other members of the expedition had to come in with the result of their day's hunt. Let us therefore turn for a little to follow their footsteps.

# CHAPTER VIII.

*Shows that too High a Price is Sometimes Paid
for Success in Hunting.*

The successful commencement of this part of the day's hunt was somewhat curiously brought about by the major.

Most people have a distinct and strong antipathy for some creature which has the power of inspiring them with a species of loathing, amounting almost to terror. Some who would face a mad bull coolly enough spring with disgust from a cockroach or a centipede. Others there are who would permit a mouse to creep about their person with indifference, but would shudder at the bare idea of a frog happening to get under their bedclothes. Now Major Garret's peculiar horror was a serpent. He was a daring man by nature, and experience had made him almost foolhardy. He would have faced a lion, or an enraged elephant, any day without flinching, and cared nothing for a buffalo-bull, however mad, provided he had a trustworthy gun in his hand; but a serpent would cause him to leap into the air like a kangaroo, and if it chanced to come at him unawares he would fly from it like the wind, in a paroxysm of horror — if not fear!

There was no lack of serpents in that region to trouble the worthy major. Numbers of them, of all kinds and sizes, were to be seen. One in particular, which Mafuta killed with an assegai, was eight feet three inches long, and so copiously supplied with poison that one of the dogs which attacked it, and was bitten, died almost instantaneously, while another died in about five minutes. Tom Brown, on another occasion, knocked over one of the same species, and it continued to distil pure poison from the fangs for hours after its head was cut off. Besides these there were the puff-adders, which were very dangerous; and several vipers, as well as many other kinds which were comparatively harmless. But the poor major's horror was so great as to cause him to regard the whole family in one light. He never paused to observe whether a serpent was poisonous. Enough for him that it was one of the hated race, to be killed in a violent hurry or fled from in tremendous haste!

This being the case, it is not to be regarded as a wonder that, when the party, early in the day, were passing a thicket out of which glided a very large serpent, the major should give a shout and incontinently discharge both barrels at it simultaneously. It chanced to be a python of great size, full fifteen feet long, and thicker than a man's thigh, but a really harmless species of serpent. The major, however, did not know this, or did not care. His shots, although fired at random, hit the creature in the spine; nevertheless it retained power to raise its head fully five feet in the air, and to open its mouth in a very threatening manner within a few feet of the major's face. This was more than he could bear. He turned, dropped his gun, and fled like a maniac, while his comrades, who had recognised the species of serpent, stood laughing at him heartily. He did not stop until he dashed headlong into a thicket, far away to the right of their line of march. Here the "wait-a-bit" thorns effectually checked his progress.

Now it chanced that in this very thicket, which would have been passed by unnoticed but for the python, there was a portly young female elephant with a very stout little daughter. Amazed at the very sudden and reckless intrusion of the sportsman, this anxious mother at once sounded her war-trumpet and charged. The major turned and fled back to his friends as fast as he had run away from them. The elephant did not follow, but the hunters, having discovered her retreat, were not slow to follow and attack her.

As they drew near, the mother elephant set herself on the danger side of her little one, and putting her proboscis over it, as if to assure it of protection, urged it to run, which it did pretty smartly. But neither of them galloped; their quickest pace was only a sharp walk, which, however, was quick enough to oblige the pursuers to run at full speed. The big one frequently glanced back, apparently to see if she were gaining ground, and then looked at her young one and ran after it, sometimes sideways, as if her feelings were divided between anxiety to protect her off-spring and desire to revenge the temerity of her persecutors. The hunters kept about a hundred yards in her rear, and as they were pretty sure of securing her, the European sportsmen held back, in order to have an opportunity of witnessing the method of attack practised by the band of natives who were with them.

Presently they came to a rivulet, and the time spent by the elephants in descending and getting up the opposite bank enabled the natives to get within twenty yards of them, when they discharged their spears at them. The old one received the most of these in various parts of her body, for she did her best to shield the young one; but the latter received a few notwithstanding. After the first discharge the old one's sides ran down with blood, and in a short time she bristled all over with spears like a monstrous porcupine. She soon seemed to give up all thought of defending her young, and began to flee for her life, so that the calf was quickly killed; but no sooner did the mother observe this, than all fear forsook her; she stopped in her career, turned round, and, with a shriek of rage, charged her pursuers, who fled right and left like a band of huge black monkeys. The elephant ran straight on and went right through the whole party, but came near no one. She then continued her flight, in the course of which she crossed several rivulets, and at each of these received fresh spears. Several times she turned and charged, but never in any ease did she run more than a hundred yards.

Gradually she grew weak from loss of blood, which poured from her like rain; and at last, when she was making a charge, she staggered round and sank down dead in a kneeling posture.

The natives were overjoyed of course at their success, and at the prospect of a baked elephant's foot for supper, and Hicks was much pleased with the tusks, which were large and valuable. He surveyed them with a complacent smile, and observed that he had much need of a little ivory like that, for the expenses of a trading expedition were very heavy.

"But you have reason to expect a good deal in this part of the country," said the major, "if all that is rumoured be true."

"No doubt there is some truth in what is reported; we shall see. Meanwhile, yonder goes something to encourage us."

He pointed towards an opening in a thicket close at hand, where an elephant was seen running towards them as if ignorant of their presence.

"Some one must be after that fellow," said Hicks. About a dozen natives emerged from the thicket as he spoke. They were evidently driving the elephant, which was a large bull, towards the hunters for the purpose of letting them have a good shot; so the latter at once hid themselves. When the elephant drew near it seemed to suspect danger ahead, for it burned to the right when at a distance of about a hundred yards. This was a great disappointment, so the major, rather than be balked altogether, tried a long shot and broke the animal's fore-leg. Then, running after him at a pace which even the supple natives could not equal, he got close up and sent a ball into his head, which stunned him; but it took four additional shots to kill him.

This was an unusually fortunate case, for elephants are not easily killed. The African elephant is in many respects different from that of India, and is never killed, like the Ceylon elephant, by a single ball in the brain. Dr. Livingstone tells us that on one occasion, when he was out with a large party of natives, a troop of elephants were attacked by them, and that one of these, in running away, fell into a hole, and, before he could extricate himself, an opportunity was allowed for all the men to throw their spears. When the elephant rose he was like a huge porcupine, for each of the seventy or eighty men had discharged more than one spear at him. As they had no more, they sent for the Doctor to shoot him. He, anxious to put the animal at once out of pain, went up to within twenty yards, rested his gun on an ant-hill, so as to take steady aim; but though he fired twelve two-ounce bullets, all he had, into different parts, he could not kill it. As it was getting dark, they were obliged to leave it standing there, intending to return in the morning in the full expectation of finding it dead; but though they searched all that day, and went over more than ten miles of ground, they never saw it again!

The female elephant killed by our hunters at this time was a comparatively small one. Its height was eight feet eight inches. Many of those which were afterwards killed were of much greater height. Indian elephants never reach to the enormous size of the African elephant, which is distinguished from that of India by a mark that cannot be mistaken, namely, the ear, which in the African species is enormously large. That of the female just killed measured four feet five inches in length and four feet in breadth. A native has been seen to creep under an elephant's ear so as to be quite covered from the rain. The African elephant has never been tamed at the Cape, nor has one ever been exhibited in England.

But to return to our hunters. Before that day had closed, the major and his friends had made good bags. The total result of the day's hunt by both parties was, five sea-cows, four elephants, two buffaloes, a giraffe, and a number of birds of various kinds.

Of course this set the natives of the kraal into a ferment of joyous festivity, and the sportsmen rose very high in their estimation, insomuch that they overwhelmed them with gifts of native produce. Our hero was an especial favourite, because, on several occasions, he turned his medical and surgical knowledge to good account, and afforded many of them great relief from troubles which their own doctors had failed to cure or charm away.

Some time after this, when they were travelling through a comparatively dry district, they encamped near a pool of water, and the sights they saw there were most amazing; for all the animals in the neighbourhood flocked to the pool to slake their burning thirst.

After supper, instead of going to rest, Tom Brown and most of the party resolved to go and watch this pool — the moon being bright at the time. They had not lain long in ambush beside it when a troop of elephants came rushing into it, and began to drink with great avidity, spirting the water over each other and shrieking with delight. For some hours the hunters remained on the watch there, and saw animals of all kinds come down to drink — antelopes, zebras, buffaloes, etc., in great numbers.

Thus they passed through the country, enjoying themselves, and adding considerably to Hicks's stock of ivory, when an incident occurred which threw a deep gloom over the party for some time.

One day they went out after some elephants which were reported to be near to their encampment, and about noon rested a little to refresh themselves. They had set out as a united party on this occasion accompanied by a large band of natives armed with spears. Just after leaving the spot where they rested, the major discovered that he had left his knife behind him, and went back to look for it, in company with Tom Brown. As it was only quarter of a mile off, or less, they foolishly left their guns behind them. On nearing the spot, Tom stopped a few moments, and bent down to examine a beautiful flower. The major walked on, but had not gone many paces when three lions walked out of a thicket not twenty paces off. Tom had risen, and saw the lions, and, for the first time in his life, felt a sensation about the heart which is popularly known as "the blood curdling in the vein." The major, being totally unarmed, stopped, and stood motionless like a statue. The lions stopped also, being evidently taken by surprise at the sudden and unexpected apparition of a man! Had the major turned and fled, it is almost certain that his fate would have been sealed, but he stood firm as a rock, and Tom observed that he did not even change colour as he gazed with a fixed glassy stare at the lions.

Unused to such treatment, the animals winced under it. Their own glances became uneasy; then they turned slowly round and slunk away, with the air of creatures which know that they have been doing wrong! In a few moments they bounded off at full speed, their pace being accelerated by the terrible yell which burst simultaneously from Tom and the major, who found intense relief in this violent expression of their pent-up feelings!

But this, good reader, is not the gloomy incident to which we have referred. It was just after the occurrence of this minor episode in the proceedings of the day, that the party came upon fresh tracks of a troop of elephants, and set off in pursuit. The Englishmen were on horseback, having obtained steeds from a trader whom they had met farther south, but the natives — a very large band — were on foot.

While they were advancing through a somewhat open part of the country, four lions were seen on the top of a low sandhill, which was covered with bushes and a few stunted trees. It was at once resolved that they should be surrounded. Accordingly, the natives were ordered to form a wide ring round the hill.

"Now," said Hicks, who assumed command of the party in virtue of his superior knowledge, "we must separate and advance from different directions, and be sure, gentlemen, that you don't shoot the niggers. Look well before you. That hollow is a very likely place for one of them to run along, therefore the best shot among you had better go up there. Who is the best shot?"

The trader smiled knowingly, for he knew that the major esteemed himself the best.

"I think I am," said Wilkins, with an air of great simplicity.

There was a general laugh at this, for it was well known that Wilkins was the worst shot of the party.

"Well, now," said he with a good-natured smile, "since you have insulted me so grossly, I think myself entitled to name the best man; I therefore suggest Tom Brown."

"Right," said Pearson.

The others being all agreed, Tom consented, with becoming modesty, to take the post of honour and of danger.

"Are we to ride or walk?" he asked.

"Walk, of course," said Hicks. "The ground is much too rough for horses."

"And I trust, Tom," said Wilkins, "that you will permit me to follow you. I am the worst shot, you know, and the worst and best should go together on the acknowledged principle that extremes meet."

This being arranged, the sportsmen dismounted, fastened their horses to trees, and separated.

The circle of men gradually closed in and ascended the hill pretty near to each other. Presently Tom Brown observed one of the lions get upon a piece of rock. The major also saw him, and being anxious to secure the first shot, fired somewhat hastily and hit the rock on which the magnificent brute was standing, as if it had got up there to take a cool survey of the field. He bit at the spot struck, as a dog bites at a stick or stone thrown at him. Next moment Tom Brown sent a bullet straight into his heart, and his tail made a splendid flourish as he fell off his pedestal!

Almost immediately after two of the other lions broke cover, dashed towards the circle of men, went right through them and escaped. The courage of the natives proved unequal to the danger of facing such a charge. A great shout – partly, no doubt, of disappointment – was given when the lions escaped. This had the effect of causing the fourth lion to break cover and leap upon a rock as the first had done. The hunter nearest to him was Pearson, who was not farther off than shout thirty yards. He took good aim, fired both barrels at him, and tumbled him off the rock into a small bush beside it.

"He is wounded," cried Hicks, "but not killed. Have a care!"

Pearson was loading his gun as fast as possible, when he heard a loud shout, and cries of "Look out!" "Take care!" Starting, and turning half round, he saw the animal in the act of springing on him. Before he could move he was struck on the head, and next moment the lion and he went down together. Growling horribly, the enraged brute seized poor Pearson and shook him as a terrier dog shakes a rat. Although stunned, he was able to turn a little to relieve himself of its weight, for the lion had placed one paw on the back of his head. Instantly the major, Tom Brown, and Hicks ran up and fired six shots into him almost simultaneously, and at a few yards' distance. With a terrific roar he left Pearson, and, springing on Hicks, caught him by the leg. Mafuta immediately rushed at him with a spear, but was caught by the lion on the shoulder, and dragged down. Seeing this, Tom Brown caught up the spear and plunged it deep into the chest of the brute, which seized it savagely in his teeth and snapped it in two like a twig, throwing Tom down in the act; but another bullet from Wilkins, and the effects of the previous shots, caused him to drop down suddenly quite dead.

It was found on examination that the injuries received by poor Pearson were mortal. As could just speak, but could not move. A litter was therefore hastily prepared for him, and one also for Hicks, whose leg was severely injured, though fortunately not broken. Mafuta's hurts were trifling, and Tom Brown had only received one or two scratches in his fall. In a short time the litters were ready, and the party returned to their encampment.

That night Pearson expressed a strong desire to have the Bible read to him, and Tom Brown, who had done all that professional skill could accomplish to relieve his comrade's suffering body, sought out from the bottom of his box that precious book which the missionary had told him contained medicine for the soul. The dying man was very anxious. As gave Tom no rest, but questioned him eagerly and continuously during the whole night about the things which concerned his soul. His doctor could not assist him much, and keenly did he feel, at that time, how awful it is to postpone thoughts of eternity to a dying hour. As did his best, however, to comfort his friend, by reading passage after passage from the sacred book, dwelling particularly on, and repeating, this text — "The blood of Jesus Christ, His Son, cleanseth from all sin." Towards morning Pearson fell into a lethargic sleep, out of which he never awoke. Next day they buried him under the shade of a spreading tree, and left him there — alone in the wilderness.

# CHAPTER IX.

## *The Last.*

From this period everything like good fortune seemed to forsake the hunters. The trader's wound became so painful that he resolved to return to the settlements, and accordingly their faces were turned southward.

But the way was toilsome, the heat intense, and the water scarce — more so than it had been on the outward journey. To add to their troubles, fever and ague attacked most of the white men, and one of them (Ogilvie) died on the journey.

At last Tom Brown, who had up to that time been one of the strongest of the party, broke down, and it was found to be necessary to leave him behind at a native village, for it would have been certain death to the others to have remained with him, and their doing so could have done him no good.

"I cannot tell you, Tom," said the major, as he sat beside his friend's couch the night before they parted, "how deeply it grieves me to leave you in this way, but you see, my dear fellow, that the case is desperate. You are incapable of moving. If we remain here the most of us will die, for I find that it is all I can do to drag one leg after the other, and I have grave doubts as to whether I shall ever get out of this rascally country alive. As to poor Bob Wilkins, he is in a worse condition than myself. Now, our intention is to leave you all the physic, push on as fast as possible to the nearest settlement, where we shall get more for ourselves, and send out a party of natives under some trustworthy trader to fetch you out of the country."

"You are very kind, major," said Tom languidly, "but I cannot allow you to leave me all the physic. Your own life may depend on having some of it, and —"

"There, don't exhaust yourself, Tom, with objections, for Bob and I have made up our minds to do it. The very fact that every day we are getting nearer the habitable parts of the world will keep our spirits up and give us strength, and you may depend upon it, my poor fellow, that we won't waste time in sending help to you."

The major's voice trembled a little, for he had become very weak, and had secret misgivings that he would never see his friend again.

"We are going to leave Mafuta with you," he added quickly.

"That's right," exclaimed Tom, with an expression of satisfaction. "If any one is able to pull me through this bout, Mafuta is the man. By the way, major, will you do me the favour to open my portmanteau and fetch me the Bible you will find there. I mean to read it. Do you know I have been thinking that we are great fools to keep calling ourselves Christians when we have scarcely any of the signs of Christianity about us, and particularly in putting off the consideration of our souls' interests to a time like this?"

"Upon my word, Tom, I agree with you," said the major.

"Well, then," said Tom, "like a good fellow, get the Bible for me, and let me advise you as a friend to make use of the one the missionary gave you. I mean to turn over a new leaf. My only fear is that if I get well I shall become as indifferent as I was before."

"No fear of that, Tom, you are much too honest-hearted to be so changeable."

"H'm, I don't know," said Tom, with an attempt at a smile; "I should not be easy if my salvation depended on the honesty of my heart. I rather fear, major, that your method of comforting me is not what the missionary would call orthodox. But good night, old fellow; I feel tired, and find it wonderfully difficult not only to speak but to think, so I'll try to sleep."

Saying this our hero turned on his side and soon fell into a quiet slumber, out of which he did not awake until late the following morning.

The major, meanwhile, sought for and found the Bible in his portmanteau, and laid it on his pillow, so that he might find it there on awaking. For a long time he and Wilkins sat by the sick man's side next morning, in the hope of his awaking, that they might bid him good-bye; but Tom did not rouse up, so, being unwilling to disturb him, they left without having the sad satisfaction of saying farewell.

When Tom Brown awoke, late in the day, he found Mafuta sitting at his feet with a broad grin on his dusky countenance.

"What are you laughing at, you rascal?" demanded Tom, somewhat sternly.

"Me laffin' at you's face!"

"Indeed, is it then so ridiculous?"

"Yis, oh yis, you's bery ri'clous. Jist no thicker dan de edge ob hatchet."

Tom smiled. "Well, I'm not fat, that's certain; but I feel refreshed. D'you know, Mafuta, I think I shall get well after all."

"Ho, yis," said Mafuta, with a grin, nodding his woolly head violently, and displaying a magnificent double row of teeth; "you's git well; you had slep an' swet mos' bootiful. Me wish de major see you now."

"The major; is he gone?"

"Yis, hoed off dis morrownin."

"And Mr. Wilkins?"

"Hoed off too."

Tom Brown opened his eyes and stared silently for a few minutes at his companion.

"Then we are all alone, you and I," he said suddenly.

"Yis, all alone, sept de two tousand Caffres ob de kraal; but dey is nobody — only black beasts."

Tom laughed to hear his attendant talk so scornfully of his countrymen, and Mafuta laughed to see his master in such good spirits; after which the former became grave, and, feeling a slight twinge of hunger, made a sudden demand for food. Mafuta rose and left the tent, and Tom, turning on his side, observed the Bible lying on the pillow. He opened it, but forgot to read, in consequence of his attention being arrested by the extreme thinness of his hands. Recovering himself, he turned to the twenty-first psalm, but had only read the first verse when the book dropt from his fingers, and he again fell sound asleep.

This was the turning-point in his illness. He began to mend a little, but so slowly, that he almost lost heart once or twice; and felt convinced that if he did not make an attempt to get out of the unhealthy region, he should never regain strength.

Acting on this belief, he left the native village on foot, carrying nothing but his rifle, which seemed to him, in his weak condition, to be as heavy as a small cannon. Mafuta went on in advance, heavily laden with the blankets, a small tent, provisions, ammunition, etc., necessary for the journey.

At first Tom could scarcely walk a mile without sitting down several times to rest, on which occasions Mafuta endeavoured to cheer him up by threatening to leave him to his fate! This was a somewhat singular mode of stimulating, but he deemed it the wisest course, and acted on it. When Tom lay down under the shade of a tree, thoroughly knocked up, the Caffre would bid him farewell and go away; but in a short time he would return and urge him to make another attempt!

Thus Tom Brown travelled, day after day, under the broiling sun. During that period — which he afterwards described as the most dreadful of his life — fever and ague reduced him to a state of excessive weakness. In fact it was a battle between the dire disease and that powerful constitution for which the Brown family is celebrated. For a considerable time it appeared very doubtful how the battle would end.

One morning Tom was awakened by his faithful attendant to resume his weary journey. He got up with a heavy sigh, and almost fell down again from weakness.

"I think, Mafuta," said Tom gravely, "that I'm pretty nearly used up. You'll have to leave me, I fear, and make the best of your way out of this wretched country alone."

"Dis a fuss-rate kontry," said the Caffre quietly.

"Ah, true, Mafuta, I forgot for a moment that it is your native land. However, I am bound to admit that it is a first-rate country for sport — also for killing Englishmen. I don't feel able to move a step."

Tom sat down as he said this, and, uttering a sort of groan, leaned his back against a tree.

"W'at, yous no' go fadder?"

"No," said Tom, with some asperity, for he felt too much exhausted to speak.

"Berry good, me say good-bye."

Mafuta nodded his head as he spoke, and, gravely shouldering his load, marched away.

Tom looked after him with a melancholy smile; for he quite understood the *ruse* by this time, and knew that he would return, although the simple native sincerely believed that his motives and intentions had been concealed with deep wisdom. Tom was not sorry to get a respite, and threw himself flat down, in order to make the most of it, but Mafuta was more anxious than usual about his companion that morning. He returned in ten minutes or so, having sat for that period behind a neighbouring tree to brood over his circumstances.

"Yous come on *now*, eh?" he said gently, regarding Tom with an anxious expression of countenance.

"Well, well," replied our hero, getting up with a sort of desperate energy, "let's push on; I can at all events walk till my legs refuse to carry me, and then it will not be I who shall have given in, but the legs! — eh, Mafuta?"

Smiling languidly at this conceit, Tom walked on, almost mechanically, for nearly twenty miles that day, with scarcely any shelter from the sun.

At night he reached a native village, the chief of which considerately let him rest in an old hut. When Tom flung himself down in a corner of this, he felt so ill that he called his servant and bade him fetch the package which contained his slender stock of medicine.

"Open it, Mafuta, and let's see what we have left. I'm resolved to make some change in myself for better or worse, if I should have to eat up the whole affair. Better be poisoned at once than die by inches in this way."

"No more kineen," said the Caffre, as he kneeled by his master's side, turning over the papers and bottles.

"No more quinine," repeated Tom sadly; "no more life, that means."

"Not'ing more bot tree imuttics, an' small drop ludnum," said Mafuta.

"Three emetics," said Tom, "and some laudanum; come, I'll try these. Mix the whole of 'em in a can, and be quick, like a good fellow; I'll have one good jorum whatever happens."

"Bot yous vil bost," said Mafuta remonstratively.

"No fear. Do as I bid you."

The Caffre obeyed, and Tom swallowed the potion. The result, however, was unsatisfactory, for, contrary to what was anticipated, they produced no effect whatever. To make matters worse, the hut in which they lay was overrun with rats, which were not only sleepless and active, but daring, for they kept galloping round the floor all night, and chasing one another over Tom's body and face. After a time he became desperate.

"Here, Mafuta," he cried, "strike a light, and get me a long feather of some sort out of a bird's wings."

The wondering native got up and did as he was commanded.

"Now, Mafuta, shove the feather down my throat. Don't be afraid. I'll give you a dig in the ribs if you go too far."

The result of this operation was speedy and complete. The sick man was relieved. In a short time he fell into a deep sleep, which lasted for several hours. After this he awoke much refreshed, and having obtained some rice from the native chief, ate a little with relish.

Next day they resumed their journey, and travelled till four in the afternoon, when the fit of ague prostrated Tom for a couple of hours, as it had been in the habit of doing regularly at the same hour for some time past, leaving him in a very exhausted state of body, and much depressed in spirits.

In the course of a week, however, this extreme depression passed away, and he managed to get along; painfully, it is true, but creditably. They were fortunate enough, soon after, to meet with a trader, from whom our hero purchased two stout horses, and thenceforward the journey became more agreeable – at least Tom's returning strength enabled him to enjoy it; for it could not be said that the fatigues or privations of the way had decreased; on the contrary, in some respects they had increased considerably.

One day, while Tom was ambling along the margin of a belt of thick wood, with his sable guide riding in advance, he came suddenly in sight of a herd of giraffes. He had been short of fresh meat for a couple of days, because, although there was no lack of game, his arm had not become sufficiently steady to enable him to take a good aim; and, being unwilling to resign the office of hunter to his attendant until reduced to the last extremity, he had taken all the chances that occurred, and had missed on every occasion!

Being determined not to miss *this* opportunity, he at once put spurs to his steed, and dashed after the giraffes at a breakneck pace. The ground was very rocky, uneven, and full of holes and scrubby bushes. The long-necked creatures at once set off at a pace which tried Tom's steed, although a good one, to the utmost. There was a thick forest of makolani trees about a mile away to the left, towards which the giraffes headed, evidently with the intention of taking refuge there. Tom observed this, and made a detour in order to get between them and the wood. This made it necessary to put on a spurt to regain lost distance, but on such ground the speed was dangerous. He neared one of the animals, however, and was standing up in his stirrups, intent on taking a flying shot, when his horse suddenly put his foot in a hole, and fell so violently that he rolled heels over head several times like a hare shot in full career. Fortunately his rider was sent out of the saddle like a rocket, and fell a considerable distance ahead, and out of the way of the rolling horse. A friendly bush received him and saved his neck, but tore his coat to tatters. Jumping up, he presented at the giraffe, which was galloping off about two hundred yards ahead. In the fall the barrel of his rifle had been so covered with dead leaves and dust that he could not take aim. Hastily wiping it with his sleeve, he presented again and fired. The ball hit the giraffe on the hip, but it failed to bring him down. A second shot, however, broke his leg, and the stately animal rolled over. Before Tom reached him he was dead.

Thus the travellers were supplied with a sufficiency of meat for some days, and they pushed steadily forward without paying attention to the game, which happened to be very plentiful in that district, as their great desire was to get out of the unhealthy region as quickly as possible. Sometimes, however, they were compelled to shoot in self-defence.

Upon one occasion, while Mafuta was looking for water in the bush, he was charged by a black rhinoceros, and had a very narrow escape. Tom Brown was within sight of him at the time, engaged also in looking for water. He heard the crash of bushes when the monster charged, and looking hastily round, saw Mafuta make a quick motion as if he meant to run to a neighbouring tree, but the rhinoceros was so close on him that there was no time.

"Quick, man!" shouted Tom, in an agony of alarm as he ran to the rescue, for the Caffre had no gun.

But Mafuta, instead of taking this advice, suddenly stood stock still, as if he had been petrified!

Tom threw forward his rifle, intending, in desperation, to try the effect of a long shot, although certain that it was impossible to kill the rhinoceros even if he should hit, while the risk of killing his faithful servant was very great. Before he had time to fire, however, the animal ran past the motionless Caffre without doing him any injury!

Whether it is owing to the smallness of its eyes, or to the horns on its nose being in the way, we cannot tell, but it is a fact that the black rhinoceros does not see well, and Mafuta, aware of this defect, had taken advantage of it in a way what is sometimes practised by bold men. Had he continued to run he would certainly have been overtaken and killed; but, standing perfectly still, he was no doubt taken for a tree stump by the animal. At all events it brushed past him, and Mafuta, doubling on his track, ran to a tree, up which he vaulted like a monkey.

Meanwhile Tom Brown got within range, and sent a ball crashing against the animal's hard sides without doing it any injury. The second barrel was discharged with no better result, except that a splinter of its horn was knocked off. Before he could reload, the rhinoceros was gone, and Tom had to content himself with carrying off the splinter as a memorial of the adventure.

That night the travellers made their encampment at the foot of a tree, on the lower branches of which they hung up a quantity of meat. Tom lay in a small tent which he carried with him, but Mafuta preferred to sleep by the fire outside.

During the day they had seen and heard several lions. It was therefore deemed advisable to picket the horses close to the tent, between it and the fire.

"Mafuta," said Tom Brown, as he lay contemplating the fire on which the Caffre had just heaped fresh logs, "give me some more tea, and cook another giraffe steak. D'you know I feel my appetite coming back with great force?"

"Dat am good," said Mafuta.

"Yes, that is undoubtedly good," said Tom. "I never knew what it was to have a poor appetite until I came to this wonderful land of yours, and I assure you that I will not pay it another visit in a hurry — although, upon the whole, I'm very well pleased to have hunted in it."

"W'at for you come because of?" asked Mafuta.

"Well, I came for fun, as the little boys in my country say. I came for change, for variety, for amusement, for relaxation, for sport. Do you understand any of these expressions?"

"Me not onderstan' moch," answered Mafuta with great

simplicity of manner; "bot why you want for change? Me nivir wants no change?"

"Ah? Mafuta," replied Tom with a smile, "you're a happy man? The fact is, that we civilised people lead artificial lives, to a large extent, and, therefore, require a change sometimes to recruit our energies — that is, to put us right again, whereas you and your friends live in a natural way, and therefore don't require putting right. D'you understand?"

"Not moch," answered the Caffre, gazing into the fire with a puzzled look. "You say we lives nat'ral life an' don't need be put right; berry good, why you not live nat'ral life too, an' no need be put right — be always right?"

Tom laughed at this.

"It's not easy to answer that question, Mafuta. We have surrounded ourselves with a lot of wants, some of which are right and some wrong. For instance, we want clothes, and houses, and books, and tobacco, and hundreds of other things, which cost a great deal of money, and in order to make the money we must work late and early, which hurts our health, and many of us must sit all day instead of walk or ride, so that we get ill and require a change of life, such as a trip to Africa to shoot lions, else we should die too soon. In fact, most of our lives consists in a perpetual struggle between healthy constitutions and false modes of living."

"Dat berry foolish," said Mafuta, shaking his head. "Me onderstan' dat baccy good, *berry* good, bot what de use of clo'es; why you not go nakit? s'pose 'cause you not black, eh?"

"Well, not exactly. The fact is —"

At this point the conversation was interrupted by the low murmuring growl of the lion. The two men gazed at one another earnestly and listened. Tom quietly laid his hand on his rifle, which always lay ready loaded at his side, and Mafuta grasped the handle of the knife that hung at his girdle. For some minutes they remained silent and motionless, waiting for a repetition of the sound, while the camp-fire glittered brightly, lighting up the expressive countenance of our hero, and causing the whites of Mafuta's eyes to glisten. Again they heard the growl much nearer than before, and it became evident that the lion was intent on claiming hospitality. The horses pricked up their ears, snuffed the night air wildly, and showed every symptom of being ill at ease. Tom Brown, without rising, slowly cocked his rifle, and Mafuta, drawing his knife, showed his brilliant white teeth as if he had been a dog.

Gradually and stealthily the king of the forest drew near, muttering to himself, as it were, in an undertone. He evidently did not care to disturb the horses, having set his heart upon the meat which hung on the tree, and the anxious listeners in the tent heard him attempting to claw it down.

Tom Brown was hastily revolving in his mind the best mode of killing or scaring away this presumptuous visitor, when the lion, in its wanderings round the tree, tripped over one of the lines of the tent, causing it to vibrate. He uttered a growl of dissatisfaction, and seized the cord in his teeth.

"Look out, Mafuta!" exclaimed Tom, as he observed the shadow of the beast against the curtain.

He fired as he spoke.

A terrific roar followed, the canvas was instantly torn open, and the whole tent fell in dire confusion on the top of its inmates.

Tom Brown did not move. He always acted on the principle of letting well alone, and, feeling that he was unhurt, lay as still as a mouse, but Mafuta uttered a wild yell, sprang through the rent canvas, and bounded up the tree in violent haste. There he remained, and Tom lay quietly under the tent for full ten minutes without moving, almost without breathing, but as no sound was heard, our hero at last ventured to raise his head. Then he got slowly upon his knees, and, gently removing the incumbent folds of canvas, looked out. The sight that he beheld was satisfactory. An enormous lion lay stretched out at the font of the tree quite dead! His half random shot at the shadow had been most successful, having passed right through the lion's heart.

*      *      *

Not long after this, Tom Brown reached the settlements, where he found the major and Wilkins, who had quite recovered from the effects of their excursion into the interior, and from whom he learned that a party had been sent off in search of himself.

Thereafter he went to the Cape, where he joined his father in business. He did not, however, give up hunting entirely, for he belonged to a family which, as we have said elsewhere, is so sternly romantic and full of animal life that many of its members are led to attempt and to accomplish great things, both in the spiritual and physical worlds, undamped by repeated rebuffs and failures. Moreover, he did *not* forget his resolutions, or his Bible, after he got well; but we are bound to add that he did forget his resolve never again to visit the African wilderness, for if report speaks truth, he was seen there many a time, in after years, with Mafuta, hunting the lions.

THE END.

www.ingramcontent.com/pod-product-compliance
Lightning Source LLC
Chambersburg PA
CBHW022050170626
46808CB00003B/1421